Precision was the hallmark of a master sniper

Once a target was selected, hesitation lasted no longer than was needed to frame the mark, steady the weapon and send death to keep its rendezvous with fragile flesh.

Bolan targeted the gunner closest to his brother and sent forty-two grams of destruction hurtling toward impact. The mobster never knew what hit him. By the time his face slapped the pavement, the Executioner was sighting-in his next target.

Chaos was in the ranks now, as the hunters realized they had become the prey.

And there was nothing left to do but die.

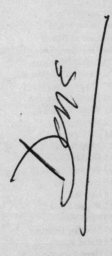

MACK BOLAN ®
The Executioner

The Executioner
Don Pendleton's®

HARD TARGETS

A GOLD EAGLE BOOK FROM

WORLDWIDE®

TORONTO • NEW YORK • LONDON
AMSTERDAM • PARIS • SYDNEY • HAMBURG
STOCKHOLM • ATHENS • TOKYO • MILAN
MADRID • WARSAW • BUDAPEST • AUCKLAND

Recycling programs
for this product may
not exist in your area.

For Major General Smedley Butler

First edition December 2013

ISBN-13: 978-0-373-64421-6

Special thanks and acknowledgment to
Mike Newton for his contribution to this work.

HARD TARGETS

The greatest danger there is today is resignation in the tendency to view the Mafia as an unavoidable evil in our time. We need to react. We need to make young people in particular understand that the Mafia, with its manufacture and sale of drugs, has exceeded itself in the criminal power that has always been its trademark…. There's a need for citizen responsibility.

—Rocco Chinnici, Former
Chief Prosecutor,
Palermo, Italy

You can't beat evil. You can only beat it down, then wait until it turns up somewhere else. The fight goes on. Involved? Hell, yes!

—Mack Bolan

THE
MACK BOLAN
LEGEND

Nothing less than a war could have fashioned the destiny of the man called Mack Bolan. Bolan earned the Executioner title in the jungle hell of Vietnam.

But this soldier also wore another name—Sergeant Mercy. He was so tagged because of the compassion he showed to wounded comrades-in-arms and Vietnamese civilians.

Mack Bolan's second tour of duty ended prematurely when he was given emergency leave to return home and bury his family, victims of the Mob. Then he declared a one-man war against the Mafia.

He confronted the Families head-on from coast to coast, and soon a hope of victory began to appear. But Bolan had broken society's every rule. That same society started gunning for this elusive warrior—to no avail.

So Bolan was offered amnesty to work within the system against terrorism. This time, as an employee of Uncle Sam, Bolan became Colonel John Phoenix. With a command center at Stony Man Farm in Virginia, he and his new allies—Able Team and Phoenix Force—waged relentless war on a new adversary: the KGB.

But when his one true love, April Rose, died at the hands of the Soviet terror machine, Bolan severed all ties with Establishment authority.

Now, after a lengthy lone-wolf struggle and much soul-searching, the Executioner has agreed to enter an "arm's-length" alliance with his government once more, reserving the right to pursue personal missions in his Everlasting War.

Prologue

Niagara Thruway, Buffalo, New York

The job should have been done by now, wrapped up and put to bed. He should have been halfway to California, having a beer in business class and trying to forget. Another less than happy ending. He was used to them. So what?

So, nothing.

Simply knowing what had happened wasn't good enough. He couldn't just fly home and tell his client—friend, whatever—that the worst she'd feared was true. He'd promised a *solution,* which meant *details.* There were ways to do a thing like this.

And doing it the right way meant collecting evidence.

Okay.

He'd done the legwork, made the contacts, asked the proper questions. It was paying off now, slower than he'd hoped for, but a person couldn't always run this kind of operation on a schedule. There were people to persuade, seduce, intimidate or bribe. A person had to cut through the crap by one means or another. Get it done.

One step remained.

Driving north, with the Niagara River on his left, he watched the signage for LaSalle Park coming up. It would have been a decent spot for his first meeting with a stranger, nice and public in the light of day, with lots of witnesses around.

At midnight, not so much.

No matter.

He was used to working in the dark, seemed to have lived in shadows for the best part of his life. He'd honed the necessary skills and knew a good Scout was always prepared.

Flying with guns, since 9/11, was a no-go if you didn't have a badge or private plane. But there were ways around airport security: reserve a hotel room and send a parcel to yourself via overnight courier. Pick up the package on arrival, at reception, and you're good to go. No reason for a hotel concierge to poke and pry, much less go looking for an X-ray scanner.

Simple.

What he'd shipped ahead was one Glock 22 semiautomatic pistol chambered in .40 Smith & Wesson, plus two spare 15-round magazines. Extra ammo was easy to come by, outside New York City, but the customized sound suppressor he'd packed with the pistol broke all kinds of state and federal laws.

The quick solution: don't get caught.

LaSalle Park fronted on the river, all seventy-seven acres of it. He'd done his homework when the meet was set, knew all about the park's pavilions, bike and walking trails, baseball and soccer fields, its off-leash dog park and memorial to veterans of World War II. He'd scoped the layout in advance and had it memorized.

While survival skills were mandatory in his business, they could take a guy only so far. The rest was instinct and determination, ramped up by audacity.

He passed the park, went on to Porter Drive and turned left, toward the river. Five hundred feet in from the thruway, he turned left again, onto DAR Drive. Daughters of the America Revolution, that would be, honored at this particular spot for no apparent reason. He drove past some kind of factory, tall smokestack on his right, into the park itself, seeking the information center, where he was supposed to meet his contact.

There it was, closed now, spotlights burning on the outside for security. He made a slow approach, the rented Camry's headlights picking out one other car. It was a newish Ford Explorer, one of the "crossover" SUVs, no one around it now, as far as he could see.

Drive on, or stop and take the risk?

I didn't come this far to take a pass, he thought, as he pulled in and killed the Camry's lights.

"HE'S HERE," Greg O'Malley said.

"I can see that," Carmine Romita answered.

"So, get ready."

"I was ready when we got here. Jesus."

"Let me take the lead," O'Malley stated.

"It's what you're here for."

"And be careful with that chopper."

"Nervous, are you?" Romita queried.

Goddamn right he was, O'Malley thought. A stranger rolling in who'd made all kinds of waves in record time, and Carmine here for backup, standing behind him with a Smith & Wesson M76 submachine gun. An old weapon, sure, but it still had plenty of kick to it, with thirty-six 9 mm Parabellum rounds in its magazine. One twitch, if Carmine started firing, and his ass was grass.

"Just watch it," O'Malley said, half snarling so his companion knew he meant it.

"Yeah, yeah."

O'Malley couldn't draw his own piece yet. He had to put on a poker face and play his part: a stoolie who'd give up the goods for cash. It played all right—at least, he thought it had—but if the stranger came out shooting he'd be caught flat-footed, pinned between two guns.

The stranger pulled into a parking slot four spaces from the Ford, switched off his lights and engine, waiting. It was O'Malley's turn.

He stepped into the light.

His contact's hands were empty as he stepped out of the shadows, moving like a former athlete who'd been out of training for a while. He wore a navy blazer over gray slacks, with a tie loose at the collar. The blazer was unbuttoned, large and loose enough to hide a gun or two.

Careful.

The new arrival stepped out of the Camry, standing with the open driver's door between him and the man who'd set the rendezvous. He'd switched off the dome light before he left the hotel parking lot, so there was no glare to distract him from inside the rented car.

"You brought it?" he inquired.

"I did. You got the scratch?"

"A grand, like we agreed."

His contact moved a little closer, frowning slightly now. "Ya know, I started thinking that it might be worth a little more."

"You said a grand, that's what I brought. There isn't any more."

"No wiggle room?"

"Well, I can get back in the car and wiggle out of here."

"Okay, already. No harm in trying, right?"

He let that pass and said, "I'd like to see it."

"Sure. It's on a CD, like a told ya."

He stood easy as the contact reached inside his blazer, braced for anything, his Glock with the suppressor screwed onto its threaded muzzle hidden by the Camry's open door. If what he saw next was a CD in its jewel case, they were cool. If not…

The hand came out, exploding with a muzzle-flash. Too hasty, and the slug zipped past him with a foot to spare. He ducked into a crouch and gave his adversary a double-tap to put him down, two hits at center mass, and he was going over backward with a stunned expression on his face.

The second shooter popped up then, blazing away full-auto with some kind of lightweight SMG. It wasn't time for dueling, so he dropped below the shooter's line of fire and let the Camry take it, aiming for his adversary's ankles, rapid-firing at a range of twenty yards or so.

The backup gunner yelped and went down hard, kept firing as he hit the pavement, but he couldn't manage aiming as he rolled, thrashing in pain. Low-flying aircraft might have been at risk, but he was open for the head shot and it silenced him at last.

Or maybe he'd burned through his weapon's magazine before the lights went out.

A lot of racket, but the park was empty and he had to check the bodies. Giving up on hope that either one of them was carrying the information he needed, he started with the first man down. He rifled the guy's pockets, quick to find a billfold that felt wrong, somehow.

He opened it and saw the badge.

"Oh, hell."

He checked the other stiff, got nothing but a driver's license. He put it in his pocket as he jogged back to the Camry. Bullet-scarred. He'd have to ditch it, thankful that he'd used an alternate ID.

He had big trouble now, and it was time to make a call.

1

Allentown District, Buffalo, New York

The neighborhood was old, settled in 1827 as Lewis Allen's farm, but it had drawn the powerful and famous over time. Mark Twain had lived there, as had President Millard Fillmore. Another chief executive, Theodore Roosevelt, had been inaugurated at the Ansley Wilcox mansion on Delaware Avenue, in 1901, after anarchist Leon Czolgosz shot President William McKinley at the Pan-American Exposition. Known more recently for its annual art exhibition, Allentown was a neighborhood of historic houses, trendy bars and artsy shops.

None of which interested Mack Bolan, aka the Executioner, in the least.

He was fresh off the red-eye from Vancouver, British Columbia, Canada, mopping up the remnants of a triad pipeline running heroin and sex slaves from the Golden Triangle to "civilized" society. There'd just been time to shower off the smell of gun smoke, make some calls to pave his way on landing, and he had been airborne, hoping that he wouldn't be too late.

And if he was? Then it became a very different game.

His flight was twenty minutes late to Buffalo Niagara International Airport, third busiest in the Empire State, but still barely awake when he landed. Customs yawned him through without a look inside his carry-on. The car rental clerk wasn't a morning person, he could tell, but she put on a reasonably sunny face for Bolan's benefit—or, rather, for the sake of Matthew Cooper, whose credit card had put a midsize car on hold.

His ride turned out to be a Mercury Milan, silver or gray, depending on the light, with a six-speed automatic transmission. It was common enough to pass unnoticed on most city streets, yet classy enough to fit in a posh neighborhood. He thought about rentals he'd trashed in the past, and bought full insurance to cover the car.

Next stop, the hardware store. Not nuts and bolts, but guns and ammo.

He was getting dressed to kill.

For what it was worth, New York State had some of the country's strictest gun laws. Permits were required to buy or own a handgun, and state police received a shell casing fired from each pistol the day that it was sold, to match against future crime scenes. Civilian ownership of automatic weapons or "assault" weapons—defined by their appearance, rather than their function—was banned entirely. That wasn't to say that any outlawed weapons were in short supply.

The opposite, in fact.

One of his quick calls from Vancouver had disturbed the sleep of Eddie Reems, a pawnbroker on Buffalo's East Side—Polonia, specifically—who moved specialty items on the side. It was a risky business, but he'd been around for years and hadn't been arrested yet. The price he charged for hardware was inflated to ensure the onset of amnesia if he took a fall. He'd put two sons through Harvard Law and kept their numbers on speed-dial.

Reems's shop, Polonia Pawn, was situated south of Market Street, close by the New York Central Terminal. On any normal day, he wouldn't have been open at the time Bolan arrived, but they'd done business in the past and Reems had always come out smiling, with a roll of cash in hand. His greeting was the same as ever, jovial but still respectful, showing off a set of dentures tanned by his devotion to cigars.

They made small talk for ten or fifteen seconds, then got down to business. Reems had the items Bolan had requested in the vault where he stored jewelry after hours. The soldier followed him in back, past showcases chock-full of everything from saxophones to faux switchblades, watches to gaming consoles. The vault was something else, bank quality, with Bolan's merchandise atop a table in the middle of the armored room.

There was one Spectre M4 submachine gun with sound suppressor and a stack of casket magazines, each holding fifty rounds of 9 mm Parabellum ammunition; one Beretta 92, same caliber, with a suppressor of its own; a Galco shoulder holster for the pistol and a gym bag for the SMG. A second gym bag was pregnant with grenades, half fragmentation, half flash-bang.

"Always a pleasure doing business with you," Reems said.

Five minutes later, Bolan was en route to the hotel.

IT HAD SEEN better days, no question. The hotel wasn't a dump, exactly, but its age was showing. Call it half a century, with hit and miss maintenance done the past decade or so. The owners wouldn't get the hot-sheet trade, so much as seniors waiting out the clock and counting nickels all the way. But there would be at least one younger guest, waiting for a visitor and running down some numbers of his own.

Bolan's first move was scouting out the neighborhood, two lazy circuits of the block as if he couldn't find the address he was looking for. An ambush didn't always show, but if it was set up in a hurry there was a better chance of someone being obvious: a watcher feigning sleep in a parked car, for instance, or a window-shopper idling too long at a store that hadn't opened yet; maybe a shadow in an alley, too upright and watchful for a junkie on the nod.

Worst case scenario, the hunters could already be set up inside the hotel. Depending on their numbers and efficiency, they could have managed it since Bolan got the call and booked his flight, but would they be that patient? If they had the target spotted, why not kick in the door and get it done?

The soldier hadn't tried to call since landing, wanted all

of the arrangements finalized before he got in touch. When it went down, there'd be no time to waste, no second-guessing or palaver. Making tracks was all that mattered. They could think about the rest of it when they were safe.

Saf*er,* that was.

Right now, he couldn't say that there was any true safe place in Buffalo. The so-called "City of Good Neighbors" could become a free-fire zone.

It had another name, as well: "City of No Illusions." Whether that was literally true—or even possible, in modern-day America—he had a feeling that some hard truth was about to hit the streets.

Hard truth and bodies, right.

But first, the Executioner was there on a kind of rescue mission. Something had gone wrong in Buffalo. He didn't have the details yet, but mortal danger had been waiting for him when his flight touched down.

Same old, same old—but with a special urgency this time.

He found a place to park the Mercury and spent another precious moment sitting there, eyeing the street. The hotel's windows stared back at him, glassy-eyed, reflecting early morning light. A hostile watcher might have studied him from every one of them, and Bolan wouldn't know the difference until he hit the sidewalk, when they sprang the trap.

He palmed his cell phone, pressed a button to connect and heard it picked up on the second ring.

"Hello?"

"Ready to check out?" he inquired.

"Damn right. Where are you?"

"Coming up in five," Bolan stated.

"No need. I'll just come down to you.

"Bear with me, okay? Double the cover."

"Sure, okay. Room 315."

"I'm on my way."

"YOU SURE THIS is the place?" Billy Scars asked.

"I'm sure this is the place they sent us," Rick Guarini

answered. "If you're askin' am I sure the guy's inside, then hell, no."

"Oughta call and double-check the address," Bobby Luna said from the backseat.

"You wanna call and tell him we forgot the address, be my guest," Billy Scars said. "I ain't about to."

"It's the *right* address, goddamn it!" Guarini snapped. "Can we just go in and bag his ass, already?"

Another fifteen seconds were lost while Billy Scars considered it. His real name was Scarducci, and the nickname was a natural, considering the two long scars along his jawline, on the left, inflicted with a razor when he'd been a punk teenager running wild around Canal Street. He didn't mind the name. In fact, he thought the scars made him resemble Al Capone, minus the flab and the receding hairline.

A name was one thing, but he still had to prove himself before he moved up any higher in the Family. This night could be his ticket if he pulled it off.

"All right," he said. "The both of you ready?"

As he asked the question, Billy Scars racked a shell into the chamber of his Ithaca 12-gauge, the short Stakeout model. He'd loaded triple-000 buckshot, just for the hell of it, six .36-caliber pellets in each fat red cartridge. If five of those rounds couldn't do what he'd come for, he still had a Taurus PT 24/7 for backup, in .45-caliber. Give the prick ten rounds of that, and see whether he had some fight left.

His two friends both had pistols, Luna carrying a big .357 Magnum Desert Eagle, which, Billy Scars surmised, might be some kind of compensation for a little gun downstairs. Guarini carried two handguns: a .45-caliber Heckler & Koch MK23, and for backup, a Charter Arms Bulldog in .44 Special, the piece that made Son of Sam famous.

One target, five guns, and…how many rounds, before anybody would have to reload?

Billy Scars gave up on the math and stepped out of the Buick LaCrosse, tucking the shotgun underneath his thigh-length leather jacket. There was no point advertising yet, before they got inside and found their man. If someone called the cops before they nailed him, it was Billy's ass that would be landing on the griddle.

They had parked across the street, an easy walk with no traffic in sight. They breezed in through the lobby, no one at reception to observe them on the short hike to the elevator—where a small hand-written sign said Out of Order. Sorry!

"What kind of dump is this?" Luna asked.

"Three-fifteen," Guarini said. "Third floor?"

"You nailed it, Einstein," Billy Scars replied, and veered off toward the stairs.

They reached the third floor, saw a sign in front of them with room numbers and arrows pointing off to either side. The gunners turned right into a musty-smelling hallway, number 315 apparently the next-to-last room down that way. And damned if Billy Scars didn't see a guy outside the door, hand raised as if to knock.

"You think that's him?" Guarini asked, half whispering, as if the tall guy couldn't see them.

"He should have a key to his own room," Luna said.

What the guy had was some kind of freaking automatic weapon, suddenly appearing in his hands and angling their way, just before all hell broke loose.

Bolan heard the shooters coming, hoped it wasn't trouble, but reached underneath his jacket for the Spectre M4, just in case. Next thing he knew, three men were standing halfway down the hall, some forty feet away, guns showing. With his finger on the submachine gun's trigger, he remembered what had brought him there, and let the muzzle rise enough that when it started stuttering, the muffled shots ripped into ceiling tiles and plaster, well above their heads.

It was enough to get them moving, back into the stairwell, out of sight. He kicked the door to number 315 and called to its occupant, "Come on! It's checkout time!"

The door swung open and a younger man stepped out, a small suitcase in his left hand, a pistol ready in his right. "How many?" he inquired.

"I saw three," Bolan said. "There could be more."

"I guess you saw, the elevator's out."

Bolan wouldn't have trusted it in any case, with shooters roaming free in the hotel, maybe an ambush party waiting in the lobby while the others came upstairs. "The stairs are covered," he observed.

"Damn it!"

"You have a fire escape?"

"Dream on."

"Okay. The stairs, then," the soldier stated.

"Listen, if we have to take them out—"

"I had another thought," Bolan said, reaching underneath his jacket, where a flash-bang grenade was clipped to his belt.

It was an M84 from the Picatinny Arsenal, five and a quarter inches long, weighing just over half a pound. Its perforated cast steel body sheathed a thin aluminum case, packed in turn with a pyrotechnic charge of magnesium and ammonium nitrate. Upon detonation, it would produce a blinding flash of light exceeding one million candela, with a thunderclap of sound between 170 and 180 decibels. The net result would be immediate but temporary deafness and flash blindness, with disorienting inner ear disturbance. Safe for use except in close proximity to gasoline or ether fumes, the flash-bang also shouldn't set the hotel's carpeting or wallpaper afire.

"You set?" Bolan inquired.

"As ready as I'll ever be."

"Okay, then."

Bolan pulled the stun grenade's primary pin, leaving the secondary pin in place but loosened, with a finger tucked through its triangular tab as they moved toward the stairs. Moving stealthily, sure, but the guys in the stairwell had to know they'd be coming. Where else could they go, except back to the room—and then what? Call the cops?

Not likely.

The soldier heard voices in the stairwell, down around the nearest landing. He couldn't catch the words, but reckoned that the shooters had to be working up their nerve to make a rush, or maybe choosing which one of them ought to risk his life peeking around the corner. That could go on indefinitely if he didn't help them out, and even with the Spectre's sound suppressor, Bolan couldn't guarantee some neighbor on the third or fourth floor wasn't dialing 911 already.

With a smooth flick of his wrist, he pulled the flash-bang's secondary pin and lobbed the slim grenade into the stairwell with a sidearm toss. It hit the farther wall, bounced off and vanished from his sight, as he crouched low and ducked his head, eyes shut, ears covered, the younger man dropping beside him as if synchronized.

Two seconds maximum on the grenade's M201A1 time-delay fuse prevented any useful defensive reaction from Bolan's intended targets. He heard a warning shout, or maybe just a bleat, before the blast eclipsed it, spewing dust into the corridor.

"We can't just friggin' *stand* here," Billy Scars was saying, with Luna and Guarini staring at him as if he might be crazy.

"Did ya notice that he's packing a machine gun?" Luna asked him, standing with his mismatched pistols crossed over his chest, wide-eyed with something close to panic.

"I got that," Billy Scars answered. "And I noticed he's a lousy shot, to miss all three of us. You pricks wanna run home and tell the boss you had to split because you wet yourself, or can we do this thing?"

"Friggin' machine gun," Luna muttered to himself. Then, louder, "Yeah, let's do it."

"Do the bastard," Guarini said, grinning with his teeth clenched, like some kind of maniac, and jiggling on his feet in some kind of crazy little dance. "Do it!"

Billy Scars was actually starting up the steps when something black and smaller than a can of soda flew into the stairwell, hit the drab wall to his left and started bouncing down to meet him.

"Grenade!" he yelped, turning to flee, and maybe took one

step before the blast propelled him headfirst down the staircase, airborne, wondering if he was dead already.

Billy Scars hit a wall and felt his nose go, flattened by the impact. Blood sprayed everywhere, smearing the wall as he slid down it, melted on the floor into a useless puddle. He was blind and couldn't figure why. There'd been a flash, oh yeah, then he had plowed into the wall. Skull fracture? Optic nerve severed?

Billy Scars thought that he was cursing, but he couldn't hear himself. There was a roaring in his ears, like what he had imagined it would be like standing underneath Niagara Falls. Jesus, if he was blind *and* deaf, he might as well be dead. He thought about ending it right there, but his damned muscles weren't responding to his thoughts—and anyway, he'd lost his shotgun on the flight downstairs.

Pistol, he thought, and tried to fumble for it, but the simplest motion nauseated him.

He tried to focus on the target, but still couldn't figure why the hump with the machine gun had been knocking on his own hotel room door. Unless—

Unless *what?*

There were *two* guys, damn it! Had to be. It was the only thing that made a bit of sense to Billy Scars's scrambled brain. He was delighted he could put that much together, then dejected in another second when he realized it didn't matter. No way he could redeem himself, share his big revelation with the boss, when he was dead.

He tried to move. Ghosts did that, didn't they? Wandered around the places they were killed, sometimes, if you believed the stories on TV and in the movies. Famous people saw ghosts all the time. If they were sober, and they weren't just lying for publicity, why couldn't Billy Scars still get a lick in while the rage was hot inside him, burning for the pricks who'd killed him?

The elevator wasn't working. That meant they'd have to use the stairs, pass by his broken corpse. But had they passed already, while his mind was churning like a smoke cloud?

Maybe not.

He heard footsteps descending. Could be other hotel tenants running for an exit, but he had to take the shot. Roaring, he pushed off from the floor and lunged to meet whoever was approaching.

BOLAN CLEARED THE HAZE of smoke and dust, saw three slack bodies huddled on the landing below him. One had hit the wall head-on and marked it with his blood, potentially a lethal injury, but there was nothing the soldier could do about it now. Only an ID check would put his mind at ease, and they were running dangerously short of time.

"Something here I want to check," he told the younger man. "Cover the stairs."

"Got it."

There were only a couple of places where they could stash ID, if there was any to be found.

Bolan's companion stepped around the bodies, angling down to watch for anyone ascending from the lobby. Three men here could mean another one or two below, for backup, maybe on their way after the flash-bang's blast, or else intent on getting out of there before the cops showed up.

The cops.

The soldier bent over the guy who'd smashed his nose and saw that he was blowing crimson bubbles. Still alive, then, for the moment. Muttering, or simply groaning in his semiconscious state? Bolan was reaching toward his open jacket, hoping there would be a wallet in an inside pocket, when the guy gave out a warbling wheeze and lunged at him.

Sort of.

It was a feeble, uncoordinated move that got him nowhere. Bolan rapped his temple with the Spectre's fat suppressor, put his lights out, and went on about his hasty search. The shooter's wallet was a fancy alligator job, or maybe crocodile. What mattered was the driver's license Bolan found.

No badge. Ditto, the other two.

Whatever finally became of them, he hadn't killed three cops.

"Okay, let's go," he said.

The hotel's desk clerk had appeared from hiding by the time they reached the lobby, but he saw them coming, calling out, "I didn't see a thing!" before he ducked into the back and out of sight.

No one else was waiting for them as they cleared the lobby and emerged onto the street, tucking their guns away. A taxi passed, its driver briefly glancing at them, rolling on when neither of them tried to flag him down.

"I'm parked across the street. The Mercury," Bolan said, as he checked both ways. Still no sign of an ambush or a spotter.

Had the Buick parked in front of the hotel delivered his assailants? Likely, since it wasn't sitting there when Bolan had entered. The Executioner guessed the driver had to be one of those he'd dusted with the flash-bang. Otherwise, where was he?

Crossing, his companion said, "You made good time."

"I caught a break," the soldier answered.

"Well, thanks for coming, anyway."

"It's what we do, right?"

"Right. Okay."

When they were in the car and rolling, hotel fading in the rearview, Bolan figured it was time to ask the question.

"All right, spill it. What's the story, little brother?"

2

There'd been no time for details on the phone before Bolan had scrambled to arrange his flight. It was enough to know that Johnny was in mortal danger, far from home, with no clear way out of it. Bolan was on the first flight he could manage from Vancouver International to Buffalo, aware only in broad strokes as to what awaited him.

The Mafia.

It felt like old home week, except he didn't have a home.

Now Johnny told the story while they rolled through Buffalo, watching the day break and the city come alive.

"So, like I said, I had this job."

"In Buffalo?"

"I know, okay?"

Johnny was based in Southern California, a beach town, self-employed as a security consultant and private investigator. Buffalo was worlds away.

"What happened?" Bolan asked.

"A local came to see me," Johnny said. "Name's Zoe Dirks. She lives in San Diego, a financial counselor. Long story short, she heard by word of mouth that I've been lucky when it comes to finding missing people."

"Oh?"

Johnny shrugged. "Five, six jobs the last couple of years. Word gets around."

"And she had someone missing."

"Right. Her brother. He's in Buffalo—or was, at least. A contractor. Joe Dirks."

"It's Joe and Zoe?"

"They're twins. Were twins. I'm not sure when to use the past tense."

Meaning Joe Dirks had to be dead, or at the very least presumed so.

"Go ahead."

"Okay. She told me they'd been talking about trouble he was having, just before he did the disappearing act. He'd been building a mall in Cheektowaga, by the airport, for a big, deep-pockets company. It should've been a sweet gig, but it started going sour. First, materials went missing. Joe reported it, and then a couple of supposed accountants show up, authorized to double-check his books. In fact, they have their own set with them, and he obviously gets the feeling something was rotten."

"Did he brace them?" Bolan asked.

"Not right away. He's lived in Buffalo awhile and knows how things work. The Mob gets into things, you know, the same as anywhere. It's part of life. Joe figures that the best thing he can do is file reports on any thefts, cover himself that way, and keep an eye on quality with the construction. Time goes by, and then a watchman catches two, three guys hanging around the job site after dark, mixing cement. They rough him up and split. Joe calls the cops again. They tell him there's a lot of crazy people out there, yada-yada."

"But he didn't buy it."

"No," Johnny confirmed. "He'd keep Zoe apprised of all this, as he went along. Next thing, he speaks to someone from the company that hired him. Nickel City Management. That's one of half a dozen nicknames people have for Buffalo, the Nickel City. Comes down from the bison on the flip side of the old Indian head nickels. Bison, Buffalo, the Nickel City."

"Got it."

"Anyway, they talk. The guy tries to put Joe's mind at ease. It doesn't work. He hires a local firm to snoop around and get some background on the company. Keeps Zoe posted while he's at it, then she loses contact with him. No one's seen or heard from him. She calls the cops and gets the usual spiel, adults are free to come and go, no signs of foul play at his home or office, nothing they can do. Meanwhile, with Joe AWOL, another company picks up the mall job. Life goes on."

"Except for Joe?" Bolan surmised.

"Then one day Zoe's in my office, telling me her story. *I* tell *her* I mostly work in SoCal, and I recommend a New York outfit, but she doesn't trust them after all that's happened. So…"

"You let her talk you into it."

Johnny shrugged. "She needed help."

"Okay."

The Bolan weakness. Not just damsels in distress, but any hapless victim.

"Anyhow, I do some research from the homestead, and I catch a smell from Nickel City Management. It's incorporated in Connecticut, which anyone can do online these days. An 'S Corporation' pays no state taxes, since the profits 'pass through' to shareholders and they're responsible for paying up, wherever they live."

"*If* they live," Bolan added.

"Exactly. Who knows? Nickel City smelled bad, so I flew here to do some more digging. Two days on the bricks, and a cop comes to see me, all puffed up and wanting to know why I'm 'snooping around.' I tell him I'm researching public records and it's none of his concern."

"Ever the diplomat."

"That's rich, coming from you."

"Long story short?"

"Yeah, yeah. So, I keep digging, and it turns out this same cop's the one who blew off Joe about the troubles at his job site. Leo Kelly, a detective, sixteen years with Buffalo PD. I hack his file, disciplinary actions, this and that. I keep offering rewards for any leads on Joe. A guy calls me for a meet, but when I show up, a couple of shooters are waiting."

"And you took them down."

"I did. Turns out one of them was a cop."

MACK BOLAN'S WAR against the Mafia began with family—his own. He'd been in military service when a loan-shark operation snared his father, and the rest was history. Threats and assaults, his younger sister stepping in to sacrifice her dignity for blood's sake, brother Johnny finding out and making the mistake of telling Papa Sam. The guilt and shame had cracked him, literally. When the gun smoke cleared at home, Bolan was orphaned, coming home to oversee a triple funeral, with Johnny in the hospital, the lone survivor.

The Executioner had spoken to police first thing, and found out that the loan sharks were untouchable. At least, within the law. Which didn't save their asses from the Executioner.

Revenge was satisfying, to a point, but Bolan quickly learned that taking out one local nest of vermin didn't solve the problem. He'd discovered in short order that the Mafia was national—hell, *inter*national—and he'd set out to tackle it one city at a time. Along that blood road, he'd made some valued friends, lost most of them in battle, and had taught the syndicate that no one was invincible.

He'd also met the first love of his life, one Valentina Querente. She'd taken Johnny in, at no small risk, and nearly paid the price when Boston's capo, Harold "the Skipper" Sicilia, learned Johnny's ID and snatched them both as hostages. You'd think Sicilia might have learned from all the misery his *amici* had suffered before him, but no. It took a Boston blitz to drive the lesson home and send the Skipper to a plot at Holyhood Cemetery, sharing space with Kennedys.

Bolan had learned something, too, from his brother's second near-death experience. The soldier had broken off with Val Querente, wished her well when she'd married federal agent Jack Gray, and adopted Johnny as her own. Thereafter, he was Johnny Gray, with "Bolan" as his seldom-mentioned middle name. The kid had thrived, gone on to college, joined the U.S. Armed Forces and seen action in Grenada and the

Middle East. At some point he'd thought that brother Mack was dead, after a fiery climax to his lonely war in New York City, but he'd later learned the truth from Hal Brognola—Bolan's link to Justice in his new life, reborn as Colonel John Phoenix. They'd been reunited in battle against San Diego's reigning Mob boss, Manny Marcelo, and Johnny had learned the hard lesson of loss once again, when his fiancée wound up on a "turkey doctor's" operating table.

History. Nobody could escape it, but that didn't mean you had to let it drag you down.

"A cop," Bolan said.

"Plainclothes," Johnny replied. "Gregory O'Malley, Buffalo PD."

"The other one?"

"Carmine Romita. He's a soldier for the Gallo Family—or was."

"That's Vincent Gallo?"

"Right. Listen, I know your rule about police."

Bolan had long ago decided that he'd never drop the hammer on a cop, no matter how corrupt or dangerous a given officer might be. Police were soldiers of the same side, in his eyes, most of them decent, even heroes. There were ways of weeding out bad apples without killing them, and he had done so on occasion.

His pledge, not Johnny's. And he wouldn't judge his brother for an act of self-defense in combat, when the enemy was unidentified. No blame, but if police were pulling triggers for the Mafia in Buffalo, Bolan would have to watch his step.

"Okay," Leo Kelly said at last. "Let's think this through."

"So, a grenade?" Detective Sergeant Rudy Mahan asked. "For real?"

"Not a frag, Sarge," Kelly answered him. "A stun grenade, I'm pretty sure."

The stairwell had a smoky smell, reminding him of fireworks more than anything. Mahan surveyed the bloodstained wall in front of him and said, "Somebody took a solid hit."

"One of the perps," Kelly replied. "The way it looks, concussion slammed his face into the wall."

"Three guys get blown up with a stun grenade, and *they're* the perps?"

When Kelly shrugged, his belly jiggled. "They were packing, Sarge. Four handguns between them, plus a 12-gauge."

"So, a hit team," Mahan said.

"They aren't admitting anything," Kelly said, "and I doubt they will. We've got them under Sullivan, regardless."

New York's *Sullivan Act,* passed in 1911, banned purchase, possession or carrying of any pistol or other concealable firearm without a permit issued by police. Each violation of the statute was a felony, bearing a potential one-year minimum sentence.

"Let me guess," Mahan said. "They're connected?"

"Oh, yeah. Rick Guarini, Bobby Luna, Bill Scarducci."

"Billy Scars? Really?"

"He did the bleeding."

"Couldn't happen to a nicer guy," Mahan said. "Are they lawyered up yet?"

"Playing deaf and dumb, so far," Kelly replied. "The EMTs took them to Buffalo General. Scarducci might stay overnight."

"Assume they ride the rap and don't say anything. We need to figure out who they were after."

"Mick's down with the clerk. You likely passed him, coming in."

Kelly was referring to his partner, big Mick Strauss. He was loud and brash, like so many detectives, but the pair of them produced results.

"This joint has…what? Five floors?" Mahan asked.

"Five," Kelly confirmed.

"Okay. Somebody dropped the flash-bang on them here, which means they had no business on the first or second floors. We need to check out everybody registered on three through five. See who's most likely to receive a kill-o-gram."

"Three floors is sixty rooms," Kelly pointed out.

"Can't be helped," Mahan replied. "Just 'cause they got blown up on three doesn't mean it was their final destination. Someone could've met them, coming down, or had a lookout standing watch."

"Jeez. It's a gang war, now?"

"We don't know *what* it is," Mahan said. "That's the problem."

"Right. You're right, Sarge."

"Was there ever any doubt?"

"Say." Kelly detained him with a frown. "You think this ties in somehow with what happened to O'Malley?"

"I wish to Christ I knew. Mob guys, again. At least there's no dead cop this time."

"Thank God, eh?"

Thank whoever, Mahan thought, and went off scowling, down the stairs.

He could go by Buffalo General and see the button men, maybe try to lean on Billy Scars a little, but between *omertà,* the concussions and whatever meds they might have pumping through their systems now, he doubted whether it would be a prudent exercise. The code of silence might not mean as much today as when his father was a cop in Buffalo, but pros like Billy Scars and company knew better than to rat on Vincent Gallo. Unless they had a sweet deal waiting at the other end…

And Mahan couldn't offer them a thing. Time off from Sullivan. Suppose they each pulled down a year for carrying. They'd be released in eight, nine months at the outside, and find a package waiting for them, in appreciation. If they'd carried out their contract, *then* got busted, that might be a different story, but the hit had literally blown up in their faces.

Funny, but he didn't feel like laughing. Not with one of his detectives in the morgue, found dead beside another Mob guy, with an automatic weapon, if you could believe it, and they hadn't shot each other. One gun for the two of them, and there was no good way to dress that up. It looked as if Greg O'Malley had been meeting with a member of the Gallo Family when someone took them out, or else—worst-case scenario—they'd teamed up to get rid of some third party who had turned the tables on them.

Jesus H. Did it get any worse than that?

Mahan thought about the scandal in Manhattan, not so long ago. Two veteran detectives had been sent away for life, both of them part-time triggermen for the Lucchese Family. It gave NYPD a black eye that would never heal, and there'd been something like the same deal in Los Angeles, a few years earlier. When Mahan thought about it, he felt sick.

Sick and *determined,* to find out exactly what in hell was going on, if it turned out to be the last thing he ever did.

BILLY SCARS WAS numb—which wasn't bad, considering. The doc had set his nose, third time he'd broken it since he was seventeen, and told him that a couple of his teeth were loose, but ought to be all right if he watched what he ate the next few days. Stay clear of apples, corn on the cob, this and that.

No problem.

All that Billy wanted was a drink or three to supplement the pills they'd given him, but he supposed the cops outside his door wouldn't approve of him imbibing while they tried to figure out what they should charge him with.

The guns, of course. He couldn't argue that one. Even if they couldn't tie him to the shotgun, which he'd try to lay on Rick or Bobby, there was still the Taurus he'd been packing when he got blown up. There'd been no chance for him to pull it, much less drop it, and they likely could have matched it to the holster he was wearing, anyhow. Some kind of CSI shit.

So they had him cold for Sullivan, maybe two counts if they took time to print the Ithaca and verify that he had handled it. Two guns, two years, if he was finally convicted and he had a tight-assed judge. Big deal.

What bothered Billy Scars the most was failing. He had been entrusted with a mission, and he'd blown it. It wasn't his fault, exactly, but try selling that to Vinnie Gallo. If you had a job to do and didn't get it done, that was a black mark on your record. If you *also* wound up getting busted, that was even worse. It didn't matter if you had been solid with the Family for years. Someone, somewhere, would start to think *What if?*

What if the cops came up with something that could send him up forever and a day. Would Billy Scars decide to rat like others had before him, going back to Joe Valachi?

Sullivan was nothing, but he thought about the guns now, knowing his were clean, but wondering about the pieces Rick and Bobby carried. Had they used those guns before? Would something turn up in the records, if the cops test-fired them and compared the slugs to others from an open case? It could get sticky then, and even though he *knew* he'd never squeal, it only mattered what his bosses thought. Would they be worried enough to take him out?

Escaping from the hospital in his condition was a pipe dream. Hell, he didn't even have the bloody clothes they'd found him in. He'd have to ask for a mouthpiece and keep asking until they brought him one. Say nothing else, beyond the magic syllables: law-yer.

He'd make bail on the charges, easy, since they hadn't got around to shooting anyone before the joint exploded. Even if they tried to blame him for the blast somehow, with nothing to support it, that was still a bailable offense. He would get out and touch base with the boss—not running straight to see him, though, in case the cops were watching him. Pick up a burner cell phone and call one of the cut-out numbers. Leave a message.

An apology.

Then start to think about the prick who'd caused him all this trouble, nearly killing him.

They had gone out hunting one guy, ran into another—he was sure of it, no doubt whatever in his mind—and got dumped straight into a crock of shit. Who *was* the second guy? Why was he knocking on their target's door when Billy Scars showed up? He hadn't flashed a badge, just started blasting at them with his damned machine gun. And the piece was *silenced,* yet.

Some kind of pro, for sure, but definitely not a cop.

Fair game, then. Billy Scars was looking forward to a rematch.

He could hardly wait.

"You still don't know what happened to the brother?" Bolan asked.

"He's gone," Johnny replied. "I'd bet the farm on that. Specifics, no."

"I guess that's not enough to satisfy your client."

"Hardly. But I've got this other problem now."

Cop-killing, right. That wasn't something that would just blow over on its own. Police didn't forget when one of theirs was killed on duty. Even if they didn't know the dead guy—or they knew him and despised him—striking one was an assault on every man and woman with a badge. It was a challenge to the brotherhood and to the public safety, all rolled into one. A blood debt that was bound to be repaid.

Toss in the issue of corruption and you made things that much worse. If there were other crooked cops in town—and Bolan hadn't seen a good-size city yet where only one or two were tainted—the surviving criminals with badges would be working overtime to hide their tracks. Meanwhile, the brass, whether corrupt or clean, would be obsessing over means of saving the department's reputation. Bolan knew the process, had observed it working from Manhattan to Los Angeles, from Dallas to Detroit. Blue walls of silence and denial, with a periodic coat of whitewash.

Then there was the Mafia. It had deep roots in Buffalo, as Bolan knew from research he'd conducted in the early phase of his one-man crusade. It dated back to 1910, when Angelo Palmeri had arrived from Sicily and set up shop, extorting money from his fellow immigrants, running backroom casinos, smuggling opium. The rest was public record, coming down from Giuseppe DiCarlo to Stefano Magaddino, Freddie "the Wolf" Randaccio, and finally to Vincent Gallo. Once upon a time, the local Family was called "The Arm," for how it squeezed cash out of Buffalo and other nearby cities.

But as Bolan had been known to prove, even a strong arm could be broken.

"You might consider getting out of town," he said.

"I might," Johnny replied.

"But you won't."

"No way."

Of course not. They were too damned much alike, that way. When the kid set out to do a job, he saw it through. And now, when he'd been cornered into cop-killing against his will, he'd want to set that right, as well. The problem was that some things couldn't *be* set right. Once they were done, there was no turning back.

"Think twice about that," Bolan said. "If police can't link you to the shooting, you're all right."

"Depends on how you mean that."

"You *know* how I mean it. No looking over your shoulder the rest of your life."

"Just the questions and doubts," Johnny said.

"Are they worse than a lethal injection?"

"Look, Mack—"

"Get out now, while you can. By the time I'm done shaking things up, they'll be looking for someone who doesn't exist."

"By the time *we're* done shaking things up."

One last try. "There's no need to get deeper in this than you are. Think of Val."

"Would she want me to quit?" Johnny queried, giving back just enough attitude.

"She'd want you to live," Bolan said.

"And I will. When this mess is cleaned up."

"It won't be clean," Bolan replied. "We can't work miracles."

"Okay. A little cleaner, then."

"And no more shooting cops."

"You know I didn't—"

"But we're both on notice now," Bolan stated. "They're in the game, on the wrong team. Some of them, anyway."

"Maybe they'll all confess and mend their ways."

Now, *that* would be a miracle. For sure.

"We start with pressure," Bolan told him. "Turning up the heat on Gallo and his Family. They'll want results, and they'll start pulling strings. Somewhere, somehow, they'll start to snap."

"Okay."

"But when it comes to lethal force, we verify the targets. How's your intel on the local syndicate?"

"It could be better," Johnny granted.

"Maybe we can fix that."

"Hal?" The prospect put a half smile on his brother's face.

"I'm not involving Stony Man, per se," Bolan replied. "But we can mine their data banks. And meanwhile…"

"What?"

"We start to squeeze."

3

Vincent Gallo lit his first Cohiba Robusto cigar of the day, holding the match an inch below its tip. Robustos contained Dominican tobacco, grown from Cuban seeds, with a Jember binder grown in Indonesia, and a Cameroon wrapper. Whenever he lit one, Gallo felt as if he were smoking the world.

But this day, it seemed, the world was trying to smoke him.

"So, let me get this straight," he said through clouds of fragrant smoke. "Since the night before last, we got one guy dead and three locked up. Plus the O'Malley thing that's gonna come around and bite us on the ass."

"It may not be that bad," Joe Borgio said.

Gallo peered at his underboss across a massive desk imported from Brazil, a block of polished teak. "You wanna tell me how it could get any worse?"

"First thing, it's one of our guys dead, not four. The others just got dinged a little."

"And arrested. Did I mention that?"

"They'll all make bond. No sweat."

"And now we're under scrutiny, because they couldn't do a simple job."

"Not all that simple," Borgio replied. "They went out hunting one prick, and they ran into another. With grenades, no less."

"That Billy Scars had better have a goddamn good excuse," Gallo said, "or he's gonna wish the prick used one of those grenades for a suppository."

"Let him talk to you, at least."

"I'll let him talk. But if I don't like what I hear…"

"This all comes back to Nickel City," Borgio reminded him. "That Dirks guy, and now whoever's looking for him."

"Speaking of whoever, how's that going?"

"We were close to him last night."

"Not close enough. You might of noticed that he got away. Again."

"We're working on it. Worked out that he used a phony name."

"Big help that is. You any closer to his *real* name? Something we can get a handle on?"

"Well…"

"That's what I thought."

"There's something else we should think about."

"Just what I need. Another headache."

"Someone helped him out last night."

"Is that supposed to be a news flash, Joe?"

"We need to work out *who* and *why.*"

"So, give me some ideas. Not local cops. The state police or Feds?"

"They wouldn't come in shooting, blowing shit apart, without some warrants first."

"Who, then?"

"Maybe…another Family?"

That thought stopped Gallo cold. "You know something I don't, this is the time to spit it out," he said.

"Nothing," Borgio replied. "But it *feels* like Family, doesn't it? Leading with the guns, I mean, instead of all the bureaucratic red-tape bull."

"You got a Family in mind?" Gallo asked.

"None in particular. But if I had to guess, the ones that overlap our interests the most are Cleveland and Detroit."

Gallo considered that. He'd spoken to Detroit's top man, Benny Matteo, just last week and hadn't picked up any kind of hostile vibe at all, which proved exactly squat, the more he thought about it. As for Cleveland, Vito Turriano had his hands full at the moment with an insurrection in his own ranks, the Fanelli brothers teaming up with the Irish to defy the old man's rules. Would he be dumb enough to risk a war with Buffalo, on top of that?

Who knew?

"You'll check on that?" he prodded Borgio.

"You know I will."

"And in the meantime, find these other pricks. The both of them."

"I'm on the case."

"And do us both a favor, will ya?"

"What's that, Vinnie?"

"Make it quick."

San Diego, California

ZOE DIRKS WAS southbound on Pacific Highway when her cell phone chirped the first few notes of "Like a Prayer." She checked the LED screen, saw that it was Johnny Gray calling, and her stomach lurched. She could have sworn her heart stopped for a second, and she started looking for an exit as she answered. She wanted to get out of traffic, just in case the news was bad.

"Johnny."

"Hey, Zoe."

"You're still in Buffalo?"

"I am. We've had some complications."

"We?"

"The case."

Her missing brother was a *case.* Of course, she knew that. It was nothing, just a turn of phrase, but still it drove the point home: Joe was *missing,* not off on vacation or a sleazy getaway with someone he'd hooked up with in a bar. Missing.

As in presumed dead.

"So, what's happening?" she asked him, forcing out the words.

"It's complicated. Basically, I called to see if you're okay."

Dirks kept him waiting, took the next off-ramp and pulled into a strip mall. She parked the Mazda in the first slot she could find and switched off its engine.

"I'm fine," she said at last. "Is there some reason that I shouldn't be?"

"No, likely nothing."

"*Likely* nothing? Sounds like something."

Johnny hesitated, then said, "We shouldn't talk about it on the phone."

"It's Joe! What's happened to him, Johnny?"

"I'm not sure, yet. He was mixed up in some things…no, that's not right. He *learned* some things, about a job that he was working, and he asked some questions. Put himself at risk."

She heard him sticking to the past tense: *learned* things, *asked* some questions, a job he *was* working. Dirks felt the earth tilt, and her breakfast threatening to make a hasty exit.

"Is he dead, Johnny?"

"I can't say that, for sure," he answered. "But you should prepare yourself."

"Oh, God. Oh, God!"

She'd known at some level, of course. Twins *knew* things, even if they couldn't pin it down precisely. No, she hadn't felt him crossing over at a given moment, like the psychics talked about on television, but she'd had an aching sense that he was gone.

"Zoe?"

She took a deep breath, held it for a moment, then released. Said, "Yes. I'm here."

"Can you get off work for the next couple of days?"

"You want me out there? Can I help you somehow?"

"No!" He spoke too quickly, and too emphatically. Covering, he said, "I just thought you should take a day or two away from home. Relax the best you can and sort things out, while I keep working here."

"There's something you're not saying."

"Zoe, listen. If your brother made some people nervous,

if they made a move against him, these are not the kind of people that you want looking for you."

"For *me?* Why would they—"

"Maybe, if they thought Joe told you something that he shouldn't have."

"I see." Not really, but the world had done another tilt. She didn't like it.

"So, if you could just go somewhere. Don't tell anybody *where* you're going. Two, three days should do it."

"Do what?"

"Be careful. Use cash, if you can. No paper trail."

"Johnny—"

"I have to go right now. I'll be in touch."

And he was gone.

Use cash? No paper trail? Some kind of cloak-and-dagger crap.

All right. She *would* go somewhere, and she wouldn't wait for anyone who might have harmed her brother to come knocking on her door. She was within a mile of San Diego International.

Screw running. She was going after *them*.

Buffalo, New York

"SOME GODDAMN PICKLE this is," Leo Kelly muttered.

"Damned straight," his partner huffed.

They were sitting in their unmarked cruiser, standard-issue Crown Victoria that any halfway savvy skell would recognize on sight and know that they were cops, parked outside a Taco Bell. Better by far than talking at the station, where the walls had ears, and even if you'd known a guy for years, you had to wonder if he might be wired.

Some goddamn pickle.

"O'Malley's fault," Strauss said. "He never should of gone out with Romita on his own."

"He didn't have much choice," Kelly pointed out.

"I mean, he should of taken us with him."

"So, it's *our* fault now?"

"I didn't say that," Strauss stated.

"Well, what *are* you saying?"

"Just that…ah, who cares. We're in the middle of it now."

And wasn't that the crying truth, Kelly thought. Stuck in the middle, with The Arm on one side, the department on the other, and a wild man running loose in Buffalo who seemed intent on turning their lives into crap.

Or maybe *more* than one guy.

"Let's go over what we know again," Kelly suggested.

"Jesus."

"You got someplace else you need to be?"

"Not me." Strauss took another bite of his burrito, red sauce smeared across his lips. Mouth full, he said, "Get on with it."

"A guy comes in asking questions," Kelly recapped. "Wants to know about this Joe Dirks character. What happened to him."

"I hear ya."

What had happened to him was a couple of bullets in the head, one each from Strauss and Kelly, after which they'd taken him to Vinnie Gallo's slaughterhouse, and Kelly didn't want to think about where Dirks had gone from there. Take it for granted that he wouldn't order any dish with meat in it from one of Gallo's restaurants in town for two weeks, minimum.

Make that a month.

"So, we try to put this nosy guy off, give him the runaround, but he keeps coming. Nothing shows up on the background check."

Meaning he used a phony name. Bill Grayson. There were probably a thousand of them spread across the States, but none had records with the New York State Police or FBI, and none were licensed as investigators.

"And so Gallo has the bright idea to take him out," Strauss interjected. "Using cops, of course."

Why not? Kelly thought, since they'd sold their badges and their trigger fingers to the Family? Having a cop take out the opposition hedged the mafioso's bets, like an insurance policy. Unless the deal went south, of course, and left you with a dead cop and a dead torpedo, plus everybody from the mayor's office to the media demanding explanations.

Giving Gallo credit, he *had* tried to clean it up. He'd traced "Bill Grayson," sent a team out to the guy's hotel to ice him, maybe swoop him up and make him disappear—but in the process, they had made things worse. Three of them had been hauled away in meat wagons, all charged with weapons violations now, and they had diddly-squat to show for it.

Except more heat.

Now all the boob tube talking heads were yammering away about a "Mob war," stirring up the public, putting heat on the commissioner to "keep Buffalo safe." It was the kind of talk you heard around election time, and didn't mean a thing in terms of real-world problems and solutions.

Sound bites. Screw them.

"We'll be up next time, ya know," Strauss said, meaning when Gallo called for help.

"Makes sense," Kelly replied. "Nobody wants this to drag on any longer than it has to."

Which was too damned long already.

"When we find this guy…"

"He's bought and paid for," Kelly said. "The prick's a cop killer. We take him out, we're heroes overnight."

Robert F. Kennedy Department of Justice Building, Washington, D.C.

HAL BROGNOLA'S PRIVATE number was exactly that: private. Fewer than thirty living people knew it and were authorized to call.

This day, the world outside his office was a relatively calm place. Not that you would know it from the newspapers or CNN, of course. Various wars dragged on, people were killing and defiling one another at their normal pace, but he was in a momentary lull between those special crises that required immediate attention from his small crew of unrivaled trouble-shooters.

And he'd known it was too good to last.

The big Fed picked up on the second ring. "Brognola."

"Striker," said the deep, familiar voice.

"Hey, pal. Good job there, in B.C. You've definitely earned some R & R."

"I wish," the Executioner replied.

Brognola felt his hackles rise, a warning sign. "What's up?" he asked.

"It's Johnny. There's a situation that's come up in Buffalo."

"New York?"

"The same."

"I'm listening."

The Executioner spelled it out in simple terms. Brognola listened, tore a sheet of paper from a notepad, laid it out beside his blotter, on the hard desktop, before he started jotting names. No point in leaving an impression for the cleaning crew, regardless of their clearance.

One guy missing, two guys dead. One of the stiffs a dirty cop.

They were like roaches, in Brognola's view. Not only vermin, but the kind that multiplied in waves. A force with dirty cops would never have just one or two. The payoff system couldn't work that way. It took corruption from the bottom to the top, protecting one another and the scumbags they were paid to put in jail. No striking revelation there, since some police had been accepting bribes and other favors throughout history. Track down the first police department ever organized, and you would find it had its share of criminals in uniform.

"I'll get the team on this," Brognola said, when Bolan finished laying out the facts. "We have a file on Gallo, obviously, and I'll ask if anybody's looking into BPD. I know there was a cop in West Niagara, convicted on a drug deal in 2010, but he went down alone."

"Blue wall?"

"I didn't pay that much attention, but you know how these things work. What's Johnny's visibility on this?"

"They've got no ID on him yet, but they'll be looking. And he doesn't want to clear the field."

"Chip off the old block, eh?" Brognola commented.

"I hope not. He's been doing all right in the real world."

"This *is* the real world," the big Fed reminded him. "The down and dirty side of it, at least."

"It needs another cleaning," Bolan said.

"Well, if there's anything that I can do to help, even if it's just running interference..."

"Thanks. I'll take whatever information you can pass along, but you should keep your distance this time."

"Okay, if you think so."

"Thanks again," Bolan said. "Later."

"Later, guy."

Brognola cut the link, frowning. He raised his pen and jotted two more names. Not targets; people he could trust for information, maybe for assistance.

"Keep my distance, huh?" he muttered to the empty air. "Like hell."

Buffalo, New York

BILLY SCARS CHECKED his reflection in the rearview mirror of his jet-black Caddy XTS while he was idling at a traffic light. He had a purple nose, taped over, and two black eyes. His top lip was a little fatter than it ought to be; his head throbbed when the Vicodin wore off. Good thing he had a source to keep it coming while his mug healed and he got beautiful again, while he was tracking down the pricks who'd handed him a steaming load of crap and then lammed out.

Bastards.

Billy Scars thought he'd smoothed things over pretty well with the *padrino*. Sure, he'd dropped the ball, but Mr. G. was understanding, to a point. He realized that the crew was sent to bag one guy, given directions to his doorstep, not expecting

some kind of commando to be there ahead of them. A guy—
three guys—could do only so much when they were under
fire from a machine gun, then some prick dropped a grenade
on top of them. They were lucky to be breathing.

But they wouldn't be for long, unless they made things
right.

Penance was the flip side of forgiveness. First thing that
they taught in catechism class: if you expected to be pardoned,
then you had to make amends.

In Billy Scars's case, that meant completing the assignment that had sent him to the hospital with scrambled brains,
then landed him in custody until his bond was posted. Nothing that he hadn't been through in the past, but this time the
arrest and injuries were incidental to the disappointment of
his boss. And if he didn't make that right, ASAP, he would
be in a whole new world of hurt.

He might even wind up as a turkey, an example to his comrades of what happened when you screwed the pooch with Mr.
G. Billy Scars had seen a turkey once. It put him off his feed
for two, three days, and that had been the point. You live and
learn, until you cross one line too many.

Then the screaming started, and never ended.

Unless they took your tongue.

First thing, he'd have to get in touch with Rick and Bobby,
get them back on board before he made another move. From
there, it would come down to squeezing anybody on the street
who might know where this Bill Grayson and his soldier sidekick could be hiding out. They obviously couldn't hide with
anyone who had a Family connection, but that still left countless options to explore.

And what if they'd already split? What if the soldier only
came to get his pal away from Buffalo? By this time they could
be down in Florida, or out in California. Hell, they could've
driven straight to Canada after the skirmish and be on their
way to freakin' Europe or Hong Kong, for all he knew.

And if he lost them, Billy Scars was done.

But something told him that the pricks would stick around.

The Grayson guy had wanted information on that contractor, Joe Dirks. He might be close, but hadn't hit the jackpot yet. He wouldn't want to go back home—wherever that was— empty-handed. Now he had a playmate who could fight, but that might also work against him.

Spotting two men on the run was often easier than tracking one.

And next time Billy Scars picked up their scent, he'd trail them all the way to hell.

"You know what this means, if you stick," Bolan said.

Johnny nodded. "Maybe it's my fate, the same as yours."

"You're choosing this fate with your eyes wide open."

"Right. Let's do it."

Bolan didn't argue anymore. His brother was old enough to make his choice, and setting him adrift in Buffalo while Bolan went his own way would accomplish nothing. On the other hand, it just might get one of them killed.

"All right," he said. "So tell me what you know about the Gallo Family."

"They run a fairly standard operation. All the usual involvements—prostitution, drugs, loan-sharking, gambling, labor racketeering, smuggling anything that you can think of in and out of Canada, and greasing anyone who needs a bribe to keep the wheels in motion. The legit side's pretty much what you'd expect. They're into garbage hauling and construction, bars and liquor stores, some restaurants, a slaughterhouse to keep them stocked with meat, pawnshops. The usual."

"The ranking hierarchy?"

"Vincent Gallo's run the Mob for going on eleven years. His underboss is Joseph Borgio, nicknamed 'The Hammer,' since he used one to collect his debts, back in the day. Across the border, Albert Cavallaro—'Alley Cat,' some call him— handles things from Fort Erie. He's kind of a de facto underboss. The Bureau files I hacked, for what they're worth, say fifty-seven members on the books, with four, five times that many known associates."

"You have the made men's names?"

"I do."

"And the specific operations Gallo owns?"

"All right up here," Johnny said, tapping his finger against his temple.

"What about a map?"

"I've got the Rand McNally street guide," Johnny answered. "It covers everything we need for Buffalo/Niagara. My last hotel had street maps of Fort Erie, and I picked up one of those."

"You go across yet?"

"No. It wasn't called for."

Switching angles, Bolan asked him, "How'd your client take the news."

"It wasn't news so much as getting her prepared to face the worst," Johnny replied. "She's definitely bright. I hope she's strong."

"You like her?"

"Not a factor."

"Are you sure? If you're pursuing this beyond the point of no return to please her—"

"I'm pursuing this because the Gallos tried to kill me. Worse, they put me in a corner where I killed a cop. That's down to them and him, the way I see it. But I don't forget. I don't forgive."

"You know there's nothing you can do to clear your name, right? You could walk into the station house right now, confess, and prove your case in court. You'd still be marked for life, with anyone you care about."

"I've got no name to clear in Buffalo. Bill Grayson did the shooting. He's retired now. Gone like Keyser Söze."

"Maybe so. But *you* aren't gone. They take you down or lock you up, the name won't matter. Win or lose at trial, you're history."

"No problem. I won't let them take me."

Easy to say, Bolan thought, but he didn't push it any further. They had plans to make, and bloody work to do, before the sun went down again on Buffalo. How many people breathing at that moment would be stone-cold dead tomorrow, or the next day?

Enough, perhaps, to get his brother clear, nobody tracking him back to his real life and his SoCal sanctuary. Failing that, if it fell apart?

Well, at the very least, they'd raise some hell before the long night closed around them.

4

Night Moves was closed when Bolan and his brother made their pass. The strip club—or "gentleman's lounge," if you bought that—opened at noon and rocked on until 4:00 a.m., two hours later than last call in most other cities across the country. In theory, that was due to the high density of industry, the city fathers granting second- and third-shift employees a chance to get sloshed with the regular nine-to-five crowd. Bolan didn't know if that was true or not, and couldn't have cared less.

What mattered to him, at the moment, was a dive devoid of paying customers.

No innocent civilians in the line of fire.

Bolan had never been a blue-nosed moralist. He thought all people should be free to drink, gamble, engage in sex for pay or pleasure as they pleased, as long as no one else was harmed along the way. He *knew* the so-called War on Drugs had been mishandled and perverted from day one, leaving America with the world's largest per capita prison population while completely failing at its stated goals. The thing he hated about "vice" was that it fed a monster.

Call that beast the Mafia, Camorra, Bratva, Yakuza, a triad—pick your country and your poison. They were all the same. It was that predatory brotherhood the Executioner despised, and if he had a chance to wound the Gallo Family by shutting down a nudie bar, well, the voyeurs would have to get their kicks some other way. Shell out for cable, maybe, like the rest of working-class America.

The two men parked and walked back to the club, Bolan's brother talking on the way.

"If anybody's here besides a janitor," he said, "my money's on Fat Augie Cappiello. He looks after things for Gallo, keeps the books, picks out the girls for dates with VIPs."

"I'd love to meet him," Bolan said.

The front and back doors to the place were locked, of course. The rear door opened on an alley lined with garbage bins, wide enough to let a truck pass for collections. It was empty at the moment except for a stray cat watching them from two doors down. The cat took off when Bolan fired a silenced round into the door's dead bolt and blew the lock apart.

Inside, they checked the place for cleaners and found no one. Augie Cappiello, fat or otherwise, wasn't around to greet them as they barged into his office, but he'd left his ledger books—one set of them, at least—for Bolan to collect. There was no time to try the safe, without a drill or other heavy-duty tools.

"What now?" Johnny asked.

"There's a menu on the wall, by the front door."

"Okay."

"Let's find the kitchen," Bolan said.

They did. It was a minute's work to snap the gas pipe underneath the grille, lower the microwave to full extension of its power cord, so that it rested on the floor close to the broken pipe, and set a can of sliced pineapple rings inside it. Bolan set the timer for five minutes and they left, jogging along the alley, slowing for the stroll back to the Mercury Milan when there were witnesses around.

They were a half block east and rolling when the place blew, spewing fire and wreckage into the street. The echo trailed them toward their next engagement.

"Think we should've left a note?" Johnny asked.

"Leave them guessing," Bolan said. "They'll get the message soon enough."

"YOU GUYS ARE late," Joe Borgio said, glaring across his table in a corner booth at Giorgiano's, with three cell phones and a spread of steaming dishes laid before him.

"Sorry, Joe," Leo Kelly said. "With this O'Malley deal, we gotta watch for tails, you know?"

"Somebody on to you?" Borgio asked.

Kelly glanced at Strauss, passing a silent question back and forth, then said, "Nah. I don't think so."

"You don't *think* so?" Borgio took a bite of sausage and kept talking with his mouth full. "Come in here, and you aren't sure?"

"You called us," Strauss replied.

Before Borgio could answer that, Kelly interjected, "It's not a problem. Someone sees us talking to you, we'll just say it was a field interrogation."

Borgio grunted. "Sitar den."

"Huh?"

The mafioso swallowed noisily. "Sit down, then," he repeated. "Christ, I get a neck ache looking up at ya."

They sat and waited while he ate, glowering the whole time. "So, are you any closer to these pricks, or what?"

"You heard there's more than one?" Kelly asked.

"What, you think we spend the whole day sitting on our thumbs?"

"No, it's just—"

"One, two, whatever. Are you any *closer?*" Borgio demanded.

"It's hard to say."

"Two of the shortest words I ever heard are *yes* and *no.*"

"You want the truth?" Strauss asked.

"Hell, no. I called you over here so you could lie to me. Of course I want the truth!"

"Okay, then. So far, we've got nothing."

"One of your own goes down, I thought you put the world on hold until you cracked the case and brought the scalps home."

"Every cop in town is working on it," Kelly said, "from

the commissioner down to the meter maids. The trouble is, our guy went down with one of yours. That's got some people worried. It makes them wonder what's been going on under their noses while they weren't paying attention. Reporters are butting in. The first place we have to look, for good appearances, is back at you and Mr. G."

"Screw that. You know damn well none of our soldiers popped your boy."

"And if we *say* that, how's it look?" Kelly asked.

"All right, all right. You got a name on one guy—Grayson, is it? How come you aren't knocking on his door, wherever he comes from?"

"The name's a phony, Joe," Strauss said. "Amazing, right?"

"Making wise-ass comments right now isn't the smartest thing you ever did," Borgio advised.

"Sorry."

A forkful of spaghetti disappeared between Borgio's lips. "Sorry's no good to any of us," he responded. "What I need from you is—"

One of Borgio's cell phones warbled at him, something from a musical that Kelly hadn't seen in years. The mafioso frowned, picked up the middle phone and raised it to his ear.

"Yeah? *What?* You're shitting me. All right. Goodbye." He snapped the phone shut, placed it almost delicately on the tabletop, then said, "Night Moves is burning up."

"Say what?" Strauss asked him.

"That's the club on—"

"We know where it is," Kelly said. "It's on fire? Right now?"

"That's what Augie says."

"A torch job?"

"How in hell should *I* know, sitting here with you two?" Borgio aimed a pudgy index finger at the nearest exit, adding, "Better get your asses over there and see what's going on."

Rising from the table, Kelly said, "We'll keep you posted, Joe."

"You'd better. With what we're paying you, I want the skinny from the inside, not regurgitated TV crap."

North Park, Buffalo

UNLIKE NIGHT MOVES, Willie G's was open day and night, year-round, except on Christmas and Thanksgiving. A plain storefront on Colvin Avenue below Tacoma, it was ostensibly a check-cashing establishment that made its profit retaining five cents on the dollar. Since the customers demanded cash, at least two burly guards, well armed, were always on the premises. You had to get past them before you saw the back-room gaming parlor: five card tables where the stakes were high and everybody kicked back a percentage to the house.

"Who's Willie G?" Bolan asked, as he parked the Mercury downrange and scanned the street.

"Beats me," Johnny replied. "Does it matter?"

"Not a bit."

They stepped out of the car, a breezy gray day suiting the jackets they wore to conceal their weapons. Bolan half expected there would be a lookout on the street, but Johnny had explained that North Park was a staunch Italian neighborhood. Most of its residents would look askance at Vincent Gallo and his Family, but few—if any—would contest an operation run with any vestige of discretion. Why court trouble, when it was so easy just to look the other way?

Going in, they showed their guns first thing. The two big guards on duty took it badly, groping underneath a plywood counter for their hardware when they should have known they didn't stand a chance. Two muted pistol shots, and they were down, twitching the final seconds of their lives away in blood, while Bolan and his brother stepped around them, toward the backroom action.

Only three of Willie G's five tables were in operation at the moment, jaded-looking women dressed in matching vests, white shirts and bow ties dealing poker underneath a cloud of smoke that hung over the scene like L.A. smog. All eyes turned toward the new arrivals, focused on their weapons, and the tableau froze.

"What the hell is this?" one of the players asked. He was a flabby fifty-something, hunched beneath a toupee that didn't fit his scalp or his complexion.

"We're collecting alms for charity," Johnny replied.

"What's alms?" the toupee man asked.

Another player said, "I gave already."

"Give again," Bolan advised. "Give till it hurts."

"It's hurting now," another whined. "I haven't won a hand the past two hours."

Bolan fired a muffled round into the middle of the nearest table, making all the chips jump. "You can keep the plastic," he informed them. "We'll just take the cash."

"You guys know who you're fooling with?" the toupee man asked. "Who owns this game?"

"I'm guessing Vinnie Gallo," Bolan said.

"You know that much, you gotta understand this is the worst mistake you ever made."

"Not even close," the Executioner replied.

"I've got the green," Johnny said, holding up an old-fashioned expandable briefcase that seemed to be full.

"Let's get the pocket money, while we're at it," Bolan said.

"You heard the man," Johnny said. "Turn them out. It's all for a good cause."

"What cause is that, again?" the toupee man asked, before he dropped a loaded money clip onto the table.

"Pest control," Bolan replied. "We're exterminating rats this week."

"Starting with Vinnie Gallo and his Family," Johnny amended.

"This is a freaking miracle," the toupee man said. "First time I ever saw two dead men talking."

Johnny swung his Glock and sent the toupee flying, while its owner yelped and hit the tabletop, facedown. Before he straightened again, his roll had disappeared.

"You want your money back," Bolan advised, "ask Mr. G. Tell him we tapped you for the new Joe Dirks memorial."

"Joe *who?*" one of the others asked.

"Just tell him," Johnny said. "He'll get the message."

"Bet your ass he will," the toupee man muttered.

"As you're leaving," Johnny said, "try not to trip over the stiffs out front. I doubt Willie G's got insurance that'll cover you."

J. Edgar Hoover Building, Washington, D.C.

HAL BROGNOLA HAD read somewhere that FBI headquarters, constructed in 1977 to move the Bureau out of the Justice building and into its own private playpen, was built in the Brutalist architectural style. He'd looked it up, discovering that it bore no relation to the "third-degree" sometimes dispensed in back rooms at police stations, but rather referred to linear, fortresslike structures made mostly from concrete. Critics said the style projected totalitarianism and urban decay, since the concrete often weathered poorly and invited vandalism by graffiti artists.

Whatever.

To Brognola, it was simply the ugliest building in town.

He'd walked over from Justice—a classical revival structure, if there ever was one—to meet his contact in person and catch some sun while he was at it. The city smelled worse than his air-conditioned office, but at least the smell was *real*.

Besides, he didn't want to talk about his problem on the phone.

Too many ears.

Jerrod Hansen was the FBI's assistant director in charge of the Criminal Investigative Division—the largest operational division, with 4,800 field agents, 300 intelligence analysts and 520 headquarters support personnel. At any given moment, his people were tracking serial killers and child abductors, street gangs, organized crime Families and corrupt public officials across fifty states, Puerto Rico and God knew where else.

He was a busy guy, but he'd made time for Brognola.

"So, Vinnie Gallo."

"Right," Brognola said. "Specifically, I'm hoping that you may have something on his ties to Buffalo PD. They had a cop killed there, the other day—"

"O'Malley, right. Went down with one of Gallo's shooters. I forget the other name."

"It's looking like O'Malley may have been moonlighting as a triggerman. That intersects a project I've been working on."

"Which is…?"

"Still classified."

The smile that Hansen showed him wasn't quite a smirk. Not yet. "No give and take? C'mon. Play nice."

"Let's say there's an operative in the area, deep cover, and the Gallo Mob was using cops to smoke him out. Maybe sent one of them to execute him…"

"And your guy got lucky."

"Hypothetically."

"I'd say he's in deep. If you don't get him out of there, they'll likely bury him."

"And suppose I couldn't pull him out?"

The almost-smirk became a solid frown. "What kind of undercover operation is this? Any way you slice it, once he's smoked a cop your boy is compromised from here till Sunday, if he tries to testify. I hate to think what any lawyer worth his Giorgio Armani duds would do with that, in court."

"It might not go to court," Brognola said.

"Whoa, Nelly. If you've got no plan to prosecute, then what…" He stopped, blinked once at Brognola, then said, "How's this? I'll see what I can dig up for you on Buffalo's finest, but I'll have to sanitize it. I can't give you anything that might expose our own people to risk or jeopardize ongoing operations."

"Understood."

"Okay. You'll have whatever I can spare this afternoon. I'll send it over with a courier."

"Appreciate it." Brognola was on his feet, prepared to leave.

"I'm thinking that you owe me now," Hansen said. Putting on his best Don Corleone, he forged ahead. "Someday, and that day may never come, I'll call upon you to do a service for me. But until that day—"

"Yeah, yeah." Brognola cut him off, already halfway to the door. "Don't quit your day job, eh?"

North Park, Buffalo

"Joe Dirks memorial? The prick said that?"

"I asked him what it meant," Lee Raimondi answered. "Piece of shit just said you'd understand."

"Which one of them was this?" Gallo inquired, speaking through clenched teeth.

"One who took the cash and clipped me on the melon." As he answered, Raimondi raised a hand to probe his wounded scalp, almost dislodging his toupee.

"I'll pay him back for that, don't worry," Gallo said. "Describe the two of them again, will you?"

Raimondi went through it one more time. Two good-size white guys, dark-haired, neither one of them appearing nervous. It was hard to memorize descriptions, sometimes, staring down the barrel of a gun.

Two guns. With silencers.

Professionals.

"You see a doctor yet, Lee?"

"Nah, Mr. G., I come straight here. I'm pissed off, more'n hurt."

"Makes two of us," Gallo replied. "I'll make good on whatever they took off you, at the game."

"Not necessary, Mr. G. I likely woulda lost it, anyway."

"Forget about it. I insist."

"Well, then…"

"And have somebody check that cut. We wouldn't want you getting brain rot, some damn thing."

"I will. Yes, sir."

When he was gone, Joe Borgio said, "Same bastards. Gotta be."

"No kidding. Where's that leave us?"

"I got people turning over every rock in Erie County," Borgio replied. "That's cops, on top of our soldiers. If they're sleeping anyplace that charges rent, we'll have them by tomorrow, latest."

"And suppose they're not?" Gallo asked.

"Huh?"

"Not renting. What if they're holed up with somebody who lives here, regular."

"Like who?"

"I don't *know* who, goddamn it! Say somebody from another Family. Maybe a cop. Maybe a Fed."

"We'd hear if this was something that the PD put together, or the state guys," Borgio replied. "The Feds play dirty, sure, but when they rob you, it's at tax time. I can't see them knocking over card games."

"That still leaves one of the other Families," Gallo said.

"You ruled out Detroit and Cleveland," Borgio reminded him.

"I might of been too quick, there," Gallo granted. "Or it could be Philly, Pittsburgh, Scranton—Christ, who knows? I wouldn't put it past Chicago."

"That's a lot of ground to cover."

"Tell me something that I *don't* know."

"Okay, Vin. I'll put some quiet feelers out. We've got at least one friend in every Family that might be trying something. Have to do it careful-like, but if there's something going on, I'll sniff it out."

"And then we'll have to do something about it," Gallo said.

"I hear you," Borgia said, sounding weary at the prospect.

"But first, we've got to find the two pricks that are breaking our balls."

"Joe Dirks memorial," Borgio said. "That was cute."

"Tells me they know too goddamn much already. If they're spreading it around…"

"That's hard to figure, Vin. The cops or Feds could maybe use it, but another Family? Why the hell would they care about some construction job in Buffalo."

"Good question, Joe. How about an answer, while you're at it?"

"Yeah. I'll add that to the list."

"Time's wasting," Gallo said. "Tell Strauss and Kelly, if they want their envelopes next month, they'd damn well better get results."

Buffalo Police Headquarters

THE WALL OF HONOR for police killed in the line of duty featured forty-six names, dating back to January 1865, when Patrolman George Dill was shot by a prowler on Oak Street. There'd been no return fire, since Buffalo's cops were unarmed in those days, but they finally caught the killer and he was hanged a year later, almost to the day of the murder.

Rudy Mahan once had memorized the names of fallen local officers, a private gesture of respect. The last three had gone down while he was on the job, one shot, two hit by cars. Now there would be a new name on the wall, and he was wondering if it would be a travesty.

Headquarters was busy as ever, a beehive planted at the corner of Church and Franklin Streets, two blocks south of Niagara Square. It hummed with feverish activity today because a cop was dead, the media was asking why a mafioso had been found beside him, and whoever pulled the trigger was still out there, raising hell. A Gallo strip club burned, and now one of his street informants had a story about two guys sticking up the high-stakes games at Willie G's. All that, on top of normal crime: the car thefts, break-ins, muggings, rapes and murders that were part of daily life in Buffalo or any other city of its size.

Sometimes, Mahan felt like Hercules, given a list of jobs that no one else could do. He'd caged and slain his share of monsters, but a couple of the other tasks hit home. Cleaning out that stable with a thousand diarrheic cattle, maybe, or fighting the hydra that grew two new heads for each one he lopped off. Try that with one hand tied behind your back, hamstrung by countless writs and regulations.

Then imagine that your own department might be rotten to the core.

It would have helped to know if he was looking for a pair of vigilantes or a hit team from some Family that wanted Vinnie Gallo nudged aside. As in the field of medicine, the remedy depended on the ailment. There was always pressure he could bring to bear on mobsters, but with dedicated crazies… hey, forget about it. They would either be picked off by Gallo's men, or go down in a blaze of psycho-glory when they met the sharp end of the Buffalo PD's response.

Either way, Mahan couldn't imagine them on trial.

Which, he supposed, would solve a world of problems.

With the perps dead, scrutiny of Greg O'Malley's sins could be sidetracked and minimized. A lone bad apple would have been removed. Call it poetic justice and move on. Don't worry about any other dirty cops.

Ignore that man behind the curtain, Dorothy.

But could he live with that?

Six years remained, before retirement with full benefits, and did he want to risk it all, bucking the whole department? Even honest cops resented those who turned against their fellow officers. Work something out on the qt perhaps, but going public was a kind of blasphemy, where law enforcement was concerned. Same thing with going to the Feds. The cop who did that would become an outcast overnight.

So…what?

Dig in and do his job, for starters. See what happened next.

But if he had to make a choice between his private honor and the Blue Code, screw it.

Let the chips fall where they may.

5

Kaisertown, Buffalo

Before proceeding into Kaisertown, they hit a pharmacy on Clinton Street for surgical masks and cheap rubber goggles advertised as safety glasses. Leaving, Johnny asked, "You figure this is good enough?"

"Should be," Bolan replied. "You don't want to inhale it or get any in your eyes. The rest can brush right off."

"Or we could charge people to snort us." Johnny saw his brother's sidelong look and added, "Just a thought."

Back in the Mercury, Bolan inquired, "You're sure about this place?"

"Two sources, plus I kept an eye on it myself," Johnny replied. "Not long, but long enough."

"Okay."

The house was south of Clinton, west side of South Pontiac Street. The neighborhood was average, some of the houses well maintained while others went to pot. Or, in the case of Bolan's target for this portion of the blitz, to coke.

It was supposed to be a cutting plant. The Gallo Family bought their cocaine from Medellín these days, pharmacy grade, 99 percent pure. Upon delivery, the drug was "cut" or "stepped on" to increase its bulk, and thus inflate the profit margin. Substances employed for cutting commonly included baking soda, different kinds of sugar and local anesthetics such as benzocaine or lidocaine. The cutting process wasn't difficult—unlike the standard meth lab, there was nothing to explode—but inhalation of cocaine during the operation could produce an accidental overdose.

So masks and goggles were needed, since the powder was absorbed through mucous membranes that included eyes.

South Pontiac was quiet as they cased the target, most of the adults at work and children off to school. The marked house was among the better-looking ones, as if the Gallos sought to mask their cutting plant with a cosmetic makeover.

So far, it had to have worked. And payoffs to the PD also didn't hurt.

"Front door?" Bolan asked.

"Why not?" Johnny replied.

They donned their masks and goggles, double-checked their guns, and left the car parked at the curb out front. After jogging up the concrete walkway to the porch and climbing three steps, Bolan squeezed off a short burst from his Spectre SMG to blast the doorknob and its dead bolt. He kicked in the door and they crashed inside.

A so-called lookout had been watching television in the front room, something about doctors from the fleeting glimpse that Bolan got. The shooter vaulted to his feet, then spun to reach the MAC-10 he'd left lying on the swaybacked sofa, but he never made it. Johnny tapped him behind the ear with a nearly silent round, and the guy kept going, taking the old couch with him as he tumbled over, out of sight.

Shouting and scrambling ensued beyond an open doorway straight in front of them. A diplomatic type stepped out, hands raised, and flicked a quick glance at his late companion on the floor.

"What's this?" he demanded in an angry tone. "We're all paid up!"

Keeping the talker and the doorway covered, Bolan heard a back door slam. The cutters were bailing out while there was time. He told the mouthpiece, "Things are changing. It's a whole new day."

"Oh, yeah? Says who?"

A Parabellum round took out the mafioso's left kneecap. He went down like a sack of laundry, if your dirty clothes could scream. Writhing and clutching at his wound, he wailed, "Goddamn it! What did you do that for?"

"To get your full attention," Bolan answered, leaning in. "Next time you talk to Mr. G., tell him that this was from Joe Dirks. Got it?"

"Joe Dirks. Jesus! I never heard of him!"

"You have now. Spread the word."

"I need a frigging ambulance!"

"Start crawling," Johnny counseled. "When you hit the curb, call 911."

Sobbing, the wounded mobster set off wriggling toward the front door they had crashed through moments earlier. Bolan and Johnny found the product laid out on a dining table sheathed in oilcloth, heaped with powder, sieves, a scale, boxes of baking soda.

"Want to try another stove job?" Johnny asked.

"It works for me," Bolan replied.

Buffalo Niagara International Airport

ZOE DIRKS WAS jumpy, agitated, getting off the plane. She'd talked to friends for years about a visit to New York, but that had meant Manhattan, not some town she'd literally never thought about until her brother moved away for work, then disappeared. She was a stranger in a strange place now, jumping at shadows, painfully aware of danger waiting for her like a trapdoor spider.

She had taken off on impulse, then had time to think about her half-assed plan while she was in the air, too late to turn around. Calling her plan half-assed was generous, in fact. The only thought she'd had, if you could call it thinking, had been rushing east to help find Joe. The warning she'd received from Johnny Gray went in one ear and out the other.

But she felt it coming back to haunt her now.

What could she actually *do* in Buffalo, to find her brother? God, she didn't even know where Johnny was, or how to get in touch with him, besides his cell phone. And a call, after he'd warned her off, would only make him furious. He'd order her to turn around and go back home, like flushing precious time and money down a toilet.

No going home, then. Not until she'd managed to do *something.* But if Johnny was off-limits, who else could she talk to?

Obviously, the police.

They'd put her off when she had called long-distance, but a worried person facing them directly might be different. Make that a worried *woman,* and she'd feel no shame at using any trick that she could think of to secure official help. Red eyes and sad demeanor? *Check.* A touch of righteous indignation? *Check.* Some decent cleavage? *Check.*

And if she got a female cop, she'd play the kinship card. A missing brother tugged at heartstrings. Play the twin card. Make whoever she was talking to believe that Joe would never just break contact, take off on a lark without at least informing her of when she'd hear from him again.

But first, she needed wheels.

Johnny had warned her not to use her credit cards, and she had paid cash for her airline ticket back in San Diego, but the rental agency wouldn't release a car without a plastic imprint for their own protection. If they dealt in cash, any palooka with a hundred dollars in his pocket could walk in, obtain a vehicle and leave, with no intention of returning it. Zoe decided there could be no harm in laying out a credit card this time.

It wasn't as if anyone in Buffalo expected her—or even knew that she existed.

But they would know, soon. And they'd regret it if they didn't help her.

After signing on the dotted line, she took the keys to a Toyota Camry, then sought out a pay phone whose directory was more or less intact. She found the address for police headquarters and consulted the map that had come with her rental contract. It couldn't be that hard to find, she thought. And if she had to stop and ask directions on the way, well, that was fine.

"Ready or not," she muttered, as she left the concourse. "Here I come."

Lower West Side, Buffalo

BOLAN'S WAR AGAINST the Mafia had started with a loan shark operation. Now, sitting across the street from G & G Finance, it almost felt like starting over.

"G and G?"

Johnny shrugged. "The Lower West Side used to be Italian, but it's nearly all Latino now. They put a Spanish twist on it. One 'G' for Gallo, one for Hector Gomez. He's the front man and recruits his muscle from a street gang called Los Carniceros. Translates as The Butchers."

"Any civilian help inside?" Bolan asked.

"It's strictly macho. All mobbed up."

"Okay. We'll leave a message if it's feasible. But otherwise…"

"I get it."

Bolan checked the block both ways, then made a U-turn in the middle of the street and parked in front of G & G Finance, saving a few steps on their exit and allowing him to watch the car more easily once they went inside. It was a small place, the counter in front covered with rippling vinyl in a faux wood pattern. Half a dozen mismatched plastic chairs stood ready for waiting customers, though none was present at the moment. At the counter stood a homeboy, hair buzzed down but not quite shaved, tattoos crawling up his neck from underneath a black-and-blue plaid shirt.

"Help you?" he asked.

"We're here to see Mr. Gomez," Bolan replied.

"He's busy. What do you want?"

A heartbeat later, he was staring down the barrels of two silenced semiautomatic pistols, still rock-steady, waiting for the new guys in the shop to show him something that he hadn't seen before. Bolan knew they had trouble when a grin broke on the guy's face, and one hand slipped beneath his baggy shirt.

They shot him blind and rushed the back room, Johnny vaulting the plywood counter, while Bolan pushed in through a swinging access hatch. The downed man offered no resistance, but it sounded as if his pals in back were scrambling for their own guns.

So much for the sounds of silence.

Johnny went in low, almost like stealing home from third, and put a muffled Parabellum mangler through the stomach of a *vato* with a sawed-off shotgun in his hands. The gut-shot banger howled; his scattergun went off and scarred a nearby filing cabinet with a spray of double 0 buckshot. A second bullet in the forehead put him down for good before he had a chance to rack in a fresh round.

Bolan was in the room by then, his Beretta spitting at the two homeboys who flanked an Army surplus desk, aiming their weapons past an older man who sat between them, hunching his shoulders and obviously wishing he could disappear. Both dropped with bullets in their heads, the second getting off a shot into the ceiling as he fell.

Which left the man in charge.

"Señor Gomez?" Bolan inquired.

He got back a reluctant nod. "That's me."

"We're taking out a long-term loan," Johnny explained. "No interest, no repayment."

Gomez answered, "How much did you need?"

"How much is in your safe?" Bolan asked, his Beretta waggling toward the aged unit in the northwest corner.

"Man, that ain't my money," Gomez said.

"That's right. It's ours."

"You don't know who you're messing with."

"The other 'G'?" Bolan suggested. "When you talk to Vinnie, thank him for us, will you?"

"Thank him?" Gomez looked bewildered.

"For his contribution to the Joe Dirks memorial fund," Johnny said.

"So, what's that?"

"Just deliver the message," Bolan instructed. "He'll get it."

"Okay. But I think you the ones gonna get it," he called after them. "I think you made a big mistake!"

Buffalo Police Headquarters

DETECTIVE MICK STRAUSS was eating a triple-meat sub—salami, ham and pepperoni, with banana peppers, onions, shredded lettuce, drenched in oil and vinegar—when the phone on his desk rang. He set the sandwich down, blotted his greasy fingers with a paper napkin and picked up the phone as it began to ring a third time.

"Strauss."

"Detective, I got someone for you," said Sergeant Flannery, on the front desk, downstairs.

"Who is it?" he asked, still chewing.

"A woman from California down here, asking for O'Malley," Flannery replied. "Name's Zoe Dirks. Something about her brother going missing."

Strauss took a second, swallowing, then said, "I'll be right down."

"Okay, then."

Hanging up, he looked around for Kelly, spotted him with Chan and Davis, by the water cooler, laughing about something one of them had said. Strauss felt the first half of his good lunch churning like a live snake in his stomach, looking for a way to come back up. He rose and crossed the squad room, plucked at Kelly's sleeve and drew him to the side.

"Joe Dirks," he whispered.

"Jesus, what about him?" Kelly asked.

"The desk called up. His sister's in the house and wants to talk about him."

Kelly processed that. He surprised Strauss with his smile. "So, let's go down and make her welcome, eh? Protect and serve, all that good stuff."

"String her along, you mean?"

"Or see if she can help us."

"Huh?"

"You think it's just coincidence, her turning up like this? Right now, with all the other shit that's going down?"

"You think she's part of it?" Strauss asked.

"Her brother *started* it."

"Well, yeah, but…"

"Let me do the talking, okay?" Kelly said, heading for the elevator.

Downstairs, they had no trouble spotting Zoe Dirks. She was a looker, with that anxious air about her worried people always have when someone else's trouble brings them to the cop shop. Strauss called up a mental picture of Joe Dirks when he'd been breathing, but he couldn't see much of a family resemblance.

"Ms. Dirks?" Kelly said, as they approached her. "I'm Detective Kelly, and this is Detective Strauss."

"Two for the price of one," she said, and tried to smile but didn't pull it off.

"We're both familiar with your brother's case," Kelly said.

"When I called before," she said, "I spoke with a Detective O'Malley."

"He's no longer with us," Kelly told her. "Murdered in the line of duty."

"Oh. I'm sorry."

"Everyone around here took it hard."

"And have you caught whoever—"

"Not yet, but we will," Strauss said.

"About your brother…" Kelly cut in. "If you'd like to come upstairs with us, we'll fill you in on what's been happening."

Which would be nothing, Strauss thought, wondering what Kelly had in mind.

The elevator took its time. While they were rising to the third floor, Kelly asked the woman, "Are you staying here, in Buffalo?"

"Just for a little while," she said. "I haven't actually found a place yet, but…"

"There are a couple nice hotels I'd recommend," he said. "Clean but not too pricey, more or less downtown. Secure, you know?"

"Thanks. That's a help."

"This is the squad room," Kelly said, as they arrived. "My desk is over here."

Kelly turned then, half smiling. "Mick? Could you get us the Dirks case file?"

"Sure thing," Strauss said, and headed off toward the bank of filing cabinets on the north wall of the bullpen, wondering who the heck put him in charge.

Willert Park, Buffalo

BOLAN DROVE NORTH along Iroquois Alley—a street, in fact, despite its name—and eyed the target as he passed. He reached Broadway, turned left, then left again onto Hickory, the next street over, looking for a place to park the Mercury.

"How many do you figure?" he asked Johnny.

"Hard to say. They own the building, but the ground floor's business, like you saw. That leaves three floors, but Gallo's bound to have most of his soldiers on the street by now. Between the planners and the ones coming off shift to catch a nap, I figure eight, ten tops."

"Scattered around three floors."

"Most likely concentrated on the second," Johnny said. "From what I hear, it's set up like a dormitory, for emergencies."

"Okay. Let's find out if this qualifies."

They parked and locked the car, leaving their liberated war chest in the trunk, moving along an alley that connected Hickory to Iroquois. At its east end, they watched traffic for a moment, then crossed over, still a block south of the target, walking with their eyes averted from it, just two guys out for a stroll. They started going into stealth mode only as they came around behind it, checking out potential entry points.

"A second-floor approach means going up or coming down," Bolan observed. "You have a preference?"

"We're less likely to run into anybody coming down."

"Agreed."

They climbed the fire escape, which was less rickety than Bolan had expected. They reached the flat roof unopposed, and entered through its access door, making their way down stairs that smelled in equal parts of old age and neglect. They met no one on four or three, but paused before descending to the second floor, where voices now were audible.

"Civilians ever hang around these get-togethers?" Bolan whispered.

"At a time like this, there shouldn't be," Johnny replied.

"Or cops?"

"I would've said no, earlier this week. But now..."

"So, flash-bangs, then," he said, handing a stun grenade to Johnny, priming one himself.

They made the pitch together, ducked back out of sight as one, eyes shut, hands cupped over their ears before the twin M84s erupted into blinding light and stunning thunder. Back around the corner, then, tracking with silenced pistols, marking targets in the haze of smoke and plaster dust. None of the soldiers present looked like cops, but Bolan hedged his bets on two who'd dressed in stylish suits, versus the rest who'd kept it strictly casual.

No badges. Nothing that resembled a police ID.

Some of them were reviving as he made a second pass among them, Johnny following. Their pistols spit at point-blank range, head shots, the writhing of their enemies still instantly. It was brutal, numbing work, but nothing Bolan and his brother hadn't done before. Thinning the ranks of their opponents, weeding out the predators.

They figured that each life they ended here had been devoted to activities including murder, rape, extortion, robbery, drug-running, human trafficking, corruption and defilement of the innocent. It didn't matter if the dead were also brothers, fathers, sons. They'd crossed a line deliberately, and had thereby judged themselves. This was the sentence, long since overdue.

And Johnny's best guess had been off by one.

They left eleven shooters sprawled in blood.

There were no living witnesses this time. If the Don of Buffalo hadn't received the message yet, he'd never get it.

Not until it was delivered personally by the Executioner.

Downtown Buffalo

THE HOTEL WASN'T much, considering, but Zoe Dirks hadn't expected much. In fact, she hadn't spared a thought for where she'd stay in Buffalo, or what she'd do upon arrival, after talking to the cops. At least the two detectives had been helpful, both exuding sympathy and steering her in the direction of her current lodgings, three blocks from Lafayette Square.

Another bill was charged to her credit card, of course, to cover any phone calls, items taken from the minibar and so on. Once inside the smallish room, Zoe discovered she was hungry, and she'd ordered up a cheeseburger from room service that pleasantly surprised her. Working on her second can of soda, the hotel's price outrageously inflated for "convenience," she could feel fatigue demanding that she rest after her hectic flight across the country.

But *could* she sleep, this close to Joe? Or close to where he had been, when he disappeared?

She thought of calling Johnny Gray, had his cell phone number programmed into her phone, but it occurred to Zoe that he'd only scold her for ignoring his advice and flying to Buffalo. The last thing she needed was a reprimand to undermine her flagging confidence. But if she couldn't talk to Johnny, who—

The tapping on her door surprised her with a sudden jolt of fear. It wouldn't be a hotel waiter coming for the remnants of her meal, since she'd been told to put the tray outside her door when she was finished.

Johnny? That hope was dashed before it had a chance to

blossom, since he didn't know she was in town, much less where she was staying.

Who, then?

Trying not to make a sound, she crossed to stand before the door, then leaned in to let one eye peer through the peephole.

And beheld the square face of Detective Strauss.

Of course, the men who'd sent her there knew where she was. And if they had some news of Joe...

She fumbled with the door's dead bolt and swing-arm security latch, then yanked the door open, glad that she hadn't started to undress for bed. "Detective Strauss, has something happened?"

"You could say that," he replied. He glanced up and down the silent hall. "You'd likely want to keep this private."

"Oh! Of course, come in."

She closed the door behind him, turned to find him well inside the room, circling the bed.

"What is it?" Zoe asked.

"Quick question," Strauss replied, still surveying the room. "You know a fella calls himself Bill Grayson?"

"Grayson? No. Should I?"

"Your brother never mentioned him? Maybe someone he met after he came to Buffalo?"

"No. I'd remember that."

"Well, shit."

The stark vulgarity made Zoe blink. "What's wrong, Detective?"

Strauss turned back to face her now. "See, I was hoping you could help us out on this," he said. "The Grayson thing."

"I honestly don't understand—"

"Well, that's the problem, isn't it? If you knew what in hell I was talking about, you could save us all a ton of trouble."

"What *are* you talking about?" she demanded.

"It doesn't matter," he replied, moving closer with leisurely strides. "The bottom line, orders are orders, right? No stone unturned, and all that crap."

Zoe tensed, preparing to defend herself against this man

who stood at least six inches taller and had to weigh twice her own one hundred thirty pounds. But when the blow came, it still managed to surprise her. It was not a blow at all, in fact—simply an outstretched hand, with something in it that resembled a cell phone.

She didn't recognize the stun gun until it was pressed against her stomach, then a silent lightning bolt raced through her body, frying every nerve, and darkness swallowed her alive.

6

Rainbow Bridge, Niagara Falls

"It used to be the Honeymoon Bridge," Johnny said, as Bolan turned from Roberts Street into the flow of traffic headed west for Canada. "That one collapsed in 1938, due to an ice jam in the river."

"No ice out today," Bolan replied. He might as well have said their trip would be no honeymoon.

"Some people talk about the Rainbow Bridge, meaning a place like heaven where dead pets are reunited with their owners."

"You've been studying," Bolan observed.

"The internet."

What Bolan knew about the real-world Rainbow Bridge was that it arched for some 950 feet across the Niagara River, four lanes of traffic bustling 200-odd feet above the rushing torrent, with two headed in each direction, east and west. Commercial trucks were banned, routed downstream to the Lewiston–Queenston Bridge, while cars, bicycles and pedestrians were welcome on the Rainbow crossing. Passing from the States to Canada, you paid a toll, but returning to the U.S. side was free of charge.

Another thing: whichever way you passed across the Rainbow Bridge, you wound up in Niagara Falls. It wasn't déjà vu or one of those hokey "mystery spots," where a guy at one end of a room looked huge, while another nearby seemed to shrink pygmy-size. Simple geography explained it, two neighboring cities identically named, with fifty thousand year-round inhabitants on the New York side, 83,000 in Ontario.

As traffic flowed across the border, so had crime. From smuggling furs and guns in the eighteenth century, to liquor during Prohibition and drugs since the Vietnam War, both sides were permeated with corruption. Mafiosi had discovered Canada during the same years when they were infesting the United States, trading freely with their *fratelli* across the invisible boundary line, sometimes feuding and staining the border with blood. Often ignored or denigrated in reports of Mob activity, the Canadian Mafia held its own despite prosecutions and deadly rivalries with Chinese triads, Japanese Yakuza and Jamaican "posses."

Niagara Falls—both sides—had been a satrapy of Buffalo's Mafia Family since World War II, if not before. An underboss—currently, one Albert Cavallaro—ran the Ontario operation for his boss in Buffalo, kicking back a set percentage of the weekly take, while handling bribes and low-level eliminations on his own initiative. For larger matters, opportunities or dangers that were crucial to the Family at large, he'd be expected to consult with his *padrino* in advance.

Al Cavallaro didn't know it yet, but one hellacious problem was about to hit his territory with the impact of a fuel-air bomb. He'd likely never heard of Joe Dirks, might have missed the news about a dirty cop named Greg O'Malley, but the situation was about to land on Cavallaro's doorstep. His godfather's migraine headache was about to spread.

Clifton Hill, Niagara Falls, Ontario

"I HEAR YA," Nino Abbandando said. "And I don't give a crap, all right? The very *least* you owe me is the vig for this week, which is right around two grand. You don't start paying down the principal, you're gonna dig yourself into a hole you can't get out of. Understand me?"

More pathetic whining came from the punk-degenerate

gambler who couldn't stay out of Casino Niagara if his life depended on it. Which it might, with the amount he owed to Nino and the Family. He let it run another fifteen seconds, then cut in.

"It's a simple deal. You borrowed money, now you owe more money. It makes no difference to me whether you *got* the money. Find a way to *get* the money. Noon on Friday, I'll be sending over my collectors for it, and you better not try ducking them. Understand?"

Abbandando cut the link and lit a cigarette. The gambler would come up with something, even if he had to pawn his wife's engagement ring. Most of his clients found a way to make the vigorish they owed, and if the principal kept floating out there, what the hell? He would take their vig forever, get his money back tenfold, a hundredfold, and never break a sweat.

He loved compulsive gamblers, wished he had a piece of the casino, but the law was too damn tight for that. No matter. Nino Abbandando made a decent living with his loan operation, keeping the degenerates in business, playing while their world burned down around them, squeezing them for vig whether they won or lost. That was the beauty of it. He was spared the overhead of running games himself. Just had to pat the losers on their backs, hand them a table stake and take control of their pathetic lives.

Jackpot.

He'd heard about something across the river, a soldier going down, but he didn't know the details. Things always ran smoother on this side of the border, a tribute to Al Cavallaro and to Canada. The two Niagaras might stand only three hundred yards apart, but Canada was *calmer,* somehow. There was trouble now and then, of course, like anywhere, with any business, but New York—even the upstate part of it—was like the damned Wild West, if you compared the two.

Smooth sailing, and he didn't envy his *amici* on the other shore.

The front door's buzzer told him someone had come in

from Falls Avenue. He heard voices out front, Carlo asking whoever it was what they wanted, and getting some kind of response. A man's voice, nothing odd about that. A minute later, there was Carlo in the doorway, looking nervous, with a pair of strangers crowding in behind him, eating up the space in Abbandando's private office.

"Carlo, what the hell is this?"

"They wanna see you, Nino."

"So, you bring them back without a by-your-leave? All right, gents, what's the deal, here?"

The mobster slipped one hand underneath his desk, where he kept a fully-licensed pistol in a quick-draw holster, mounted in the knee well, within easy reach when he was seated. It was a Heckler & Koch USP, chambered in .45 ACP, never fired except on the range when he'd qualified for his permit.

The taller, older-looking of the two intruders shoved Carlo aside, and both of them showed Abbandando pistols tipped with sound suppressors. "The deal," he said, "is this. Go for your piece, or roll your chair back to the safe and crack it for us. Either way, it's your call."

Abbandando figured he had about two seconds to decide.

He chose to live.

Hamlin Park, Buffalo, New York

"She's in the bag," Leo Kelly said, casting nervous glances up and down Jefferson Avenue while speaking on his cell.

"And she's okay," Joe Borgio replied. He wasn't asking; he was telling him she'd *better* damn well be okay, as ordered.

"Sure, sure. Mick just goosed her with a little voltage. Nothing to it."

"Where's she stashed?"

"An East Side place we use sometimes, for this and that."

"Who's babysitting her?"

"Mick's over there right now."

"You warned him about any funny business?"

"Yeah, of course. He's over that, I think."

"What kinda freak gets *over* it?" the underboss demanded.

"Hey, I mean, he works it out with hookers, 'kay? Besides, I'm hoping we can borrow one or two of your guys, since they'll miss us pretty quick."

"Hmm. I'll see what I can do. Give me the address there."

Kelly named the street and gave a number. "Up by Humboldt Park, there."

"I have people who can find it. And I have some who can find your partner, if he gives us damaged goods."

"I'm telling you, he's cool."

"You give your word, you better hope so."

"What's the difference, anyhow?" Kelly asked. "She can finger Mick, which brings it back to me."

"Not that you'd ever rat, eh?"

Kelly felt a sudden dry-ice chill along his spine. "What the hell? You kidding me, or what? You think I'm freaking *crazy,* Joe?"

"I hope not, buddy boy, for all our sakes. You know the reach we got, that Witness Security deal ain't half as safe as TV makes it out to be."

"I'm not a rat, goddamn it!"

"Good thing for you I believe that."

"So, then…what's the deal?"

"You know we've come up empty, looking for this Grayson prick, plus whoever in hell is helping him."

"Sure." He nodded, even though the mafioso couldn't see him.

"And the city's *finest* ain't accomplished squat in that direction, am I right?"

"Nothing so far."

"So, if this Grayson knew Joe Dirks, maybe he knows the sister. Maybe if he finds out that she's got her little titty in a ringer, he'd come riding to the rescue. Check her cell phone. If she has a contact number, give it a ring."

"Hey, yeah. That's a good idea."

"Don't sell me short. Lots of guys have, and that was the last mistake they ever made."

"I hear ya."

"And I hope you're listening."

"Well, sure."

"If I was you, next call I made would be to check in on your partner. Make damn sure he's behaving himself with the twist. Bait's no good if it's been all chewed over."

"I'll call him, soon as we get off the line."

"That's now," Borgio said. "I'll get back to ya." He cut the link before Kelly could say another word.

JESUS. HE DIDN'T like Joe Borgio fretting, since it meant that Mr. G. was agitated, too. They both knew Mick had a little problem with the ladies, that he lost control and roughed them up sometimes.

But it had to stop when Mr. G. expressed dissatisfaction with the situation, sure. Or else he might reach down, swat Mick Strauss like a fly, and maybe step on Kelly for good measure.

Best to check and make sure that the sister was all right.

Or still alive, at least.

Falls View, Niagara Falls, Ontario

"WHAT ARE WE talking, when you say a 'high-class' brothel?" Bolan asked.

"Expensive, clean, protected," Johnny said, watching the shops roll past as they drove east on Dunn Street. "Just right for whales who want a little break from the casino action."

Which could mean the nearby Fallsview Casino Resort, Casino Niagara or Seneca Niagara Casino—all squeaky-clean and scrutinized six ways from Sunday by authorities, but teeming with the types who might've gotten used to working girls served up on platters in Atlantic City, say, or Vegas. That was where the Mafia stepped in, with women, outlawed stimulants, a timely loan for losers who were certain they could win it back, if only someone staked them to another shot.

Good times.

"Are we close?" Bolan asked.

"Take the next right, onto Drummond. Then another right, on Dixon."

Bolan boxed the block, and Johnny pointed to a reasonably stately house set back from Dixon on a deep lot with well-tended grass.

"And here we are."

"Open for trade?"

"From what I hear, they never close."

Bolan turned in, followed the driveway to a turnaround that let him point the Mercury back toward the street. Better for hasty exits.

"I suppose we're underdressed," Johnny said.

"But at least we're well-equipped," Bolan replied, slipping the Spectre M4 underneath his raincoat as he stepped out of the car.

A modern version of a madam answered the doorbell's melodic chimes. She could have been a runway model, maybe ten, twelve years ago, and still possessed the necessary poise. In line with Johnny's observation, she surveyed their outfits, saw they weren't exactly putting on the Ritz, and arched a well-plucked eyebrow as she asked them, "Can I help you gentlemen?"

"We're here about the renovation," Bolan said.

"Excuse me?"

"The remodeling," Johnny added.

"I'm afraid you have the wrong address."

"Nobody told you?" Bolan asked.

"Told me *what?*"

"You're closing down," Johnny said, as he let her see his pistol.

They pushed past her, rude but tired of wasting precious time. The foyer had a vaguely French motif, though Bolan couldn't name the style. "It's time to hit the panic button," he informed their hostess.

She was blinking at him, dumbstruck by the SMG he'd drawn from underneath his coat.

"The warning signal for a raid," Johnny reminded her. "Hop to it, will you?"

Sluggishly, as if in shock, she turned and punched a button nearly hidden by the pattern of the wallpaper. At once, a blaring klaxon sounded through the big house, followed swiftly by the noise of running feet and slamming doors. Women and men, most of them nude or caught midway through stripping, scrambled out of upstairs rooms, bustled along the second-story landings and stampeded down the curving double staircase, bolting for the nearest exit.

Two of them were slower, fully dressed and armed—one with a pistol, while his sidekick held a stubby shotgun. Bolan caught them both before they had a chance to mark their targets, stitched them left to right and back again, a dozen of the Spectre's fifty rounds dropping the pair together in a flaccid tangle.

With a shriek, the madam bolted, joined the exodus and vanished in a headlong sprint toward Dixon Street. Another moment, and they had the stylish cathouse to themselves.

"Those tapestries look flammable," Johnny observed.

Bolan smiled and said, "I wouldn't be surprised."

Calaguiro Estates, Niagara Falls, Ontario

"WHAT DO YOU mean, a total loss?" Al Cavallaro felt as if his head was going to explode. His knuckles ached from strangling the telephone handset.

"I talked to the fire captain, boss," said the voice in his ear, nervous sounding, with reason.

"Jesus Christ! Where's Monica?"

"I got her here, boss."

"Wrong. You bring her *here,* to me. I wanna hear the rest of this direct from her."

He slammed the phone down, turning back to Nino Abbandando in his not-so-easy chair, facing the bulk of Cavallaro's desk.

"Looks like you're not the only one who screwed a pooch today, Nino."

"I swear to God, Al—"

"Save it! This ain't church, and when I hear confessions, I don't hand out Hail Marys."

"What I mean is—"

"You and Carlo, up against two other guys. I make that even money," Cavallaro said. "And both of you were packing."

"So were they," Abbandando replied. "With a machine gun, no less."

"I don't care if they walked in there with a bazooka and a flamethrower. You coulda *tried* to save my goddamn money!"

It was getting through to Abbandando that the money mattered more than he did. "I don't know what to tell you, boss," he muttered.

Cavallaro spit it back at him. "*I don't know what to tell you, boss.* How about you tell me how you're gonna pay me back three-quarters of a million dollars?"

"Um…"

"And now I get a call that two guys just torched Monica's funhouse. A total loss, the fire department says."

"Hey, Al, you think it was the same two pricks?"

"I *hope* so, Nino. Otherwise, I got four guys kicking my ass, and maybe more, besides."

"I know I let you down," Abbandando said. "But if you let me have a second chance, I'll take those guys and—"

"Save it, will you?" Cavallaro interrupted him. "You run a decent operation, Nino. But a soldier? Not so much."

"I got a reputation to uphold!"

"And it's on shaky ground right now. You wanna save it, get your ass out there and squeeze those suckers you got dangling on the hook. I want my friggin' money back!"

"Okay. I'm on it!" Abbandando hurried for the door, before his second chance was snatched away.

Now it was Cavallaro's turn to take his medicine. He had to call his boss in Buffalo, brief Mr. G. on what was happening and how his people had already dropped the ball—not once, but twice. Three-quarters of a million dollars out the door, and now the cathouse up in smoke, with all the nasty questions it was bound to raise once arson dicks and the Ontario Provincial Police started sniffing around. Close scrutiny was the last thing that he needed, and the last thing his *padrino* would desire.

He buzzed for Elio Mangano, spitting orders like an auctioneer the moment that his number two came through the office door. "Double the soldiers we got on the street and tell them no one sleeps or takes a dump until these bastards are brought to me! I mean right now! Alive, if possible, or else with proof they didn't grab some *figli di puttana* off the streets and try to run one past me. How in hell you think it looks to Vinnie, when we get our asses kicked like this?"

Mangano shrugged and said, "I hear he has some problems of his own. Could be the same problem, for all we know."

"And if that's true, it helps us all the more to clean it up, eh? Show him that we're not just playing second string out here, with the Canucks."

"I hear you, Al."

"You do? One question, then—why the hell are you still standing there?"

Konica Minolta Tower Centre, Niagara Falls, Ontario

"Another day, another loan shark," Johnny said.

"They make the world go 'round," Bolan answered, piloting the Mercury around a crowded parking lot, seeking the nearest space that he could find to Golden Horseshoe Pawn & Loans.

"And when we tap them, Vinnie Gallo squeals," Johnny acknowledged, completing the thought.

It was a simple law of nature: hit your adversary where it hurt the most, to bring him down.

Golden Horseshoe took its name from Horseshoe Falls, part of the system collectively known as Niagara Falls, which also included American Falls and the smaller Bridal Veil Falls. Most people on the U.S. side were unaware that three falls went together—or if they'd been told at some point, they had probably forgotten it.

The two men's target, operated by a parasite named Peter Deodato, stood in the shadow of the Konica Minolta Tower, a 325-foot observation point for Horseshoe Falls that featured a hotel, a restaurant and a wedding chapel. Sprawling out around its base were offices, branch banks, arcades and Deodato's shop, ready around the clock to "help" some idiot who'd bet the farm and lost it at the nearby Fallsview Casino.

"Same drill?" Bolan asked.

"Suits me," Johnny replied—and then his cell phone rang. He checked the LED display and said, "Hang on a sec. It's Zoe Dirks."

He answered, "Zoe?"

A male voice told him, "Zoe can't come out and play right now. She's all tied up."

Johnny swallowed the lump that came from nowhere, threatening to block his windpipe. He put on the phone speaker so that his brother could listen in, before he asked, "Who am I talking to?"

"Names aren't important, are they, Mr. *Grayson?*"

"Okay, then. What do you want?"

"It's funny you should ask. First thing, this shit that you've been pulling has to stop."

"Which shit is that?"

"All of it, smartass! Asking about things that don't concern you. Poking into other people's business. Causing trouble for an old, established Family."

"Meaning the Gallo Family."

"See, there you go with names again. You need to focus on priorities."

"Explain them to me."

"Take this little honey that I'm looking at right now, for instance. Pretty cute there, in her birthday suit, but she could have an accident, you know? All kinds of accidents, in fact. Over and over, like."

"And you'll release her if I leave the Gallo Family alone?"

"Whoa, pardner! Not so fast. Stopping your shit is one thing, but you've caused a lot of damage, too. I figure you owe repercussions."

Johnny frowned at his brother, who'd raised an eyebrow.

"Repercussions? You mean *reparations?*"

"I mean payback, smartass. Is that plain enough?"

"What did you have in mind?"

"You and your butt-buddy come in, white flag, surrender, all that. We'll see what happens next."

Johnny gave that the full consideration it deserved, then said, "No, thanks. I pass." He cut off the call, then switched off his phone, to prevent a call-back.

"Only way to play it," his brother said.

"Right."

"It's fifty-fifty that she's dead already. If she's not—"

"I know. The only way to help her is a blitz."

The same thing the Executioner had done when Johnny had been taken hostage as a youth, together with his soon-to-be adoptive mother. Set the punks' house of misery on fire and find out if they were smart enough to bail before the roof fell down on top of them.

And maybe, in the midst of it, rescue an innocent.

7

East Side, Buffalo, New York

"Son of a bitch hung up on me!" Leo Kelly said.

"Call him back," Mick Strauss replied.

Fuming with anger, Kelly tried. "Son of a bitch turned off his phone!"

Strauss frowned. "Maybe you dialed it wrong."

"Goddamn it, he's on speed-dial. It's one button. You *can't* dial it wrong!"

"Huh. Well…"

"He has to know we've got her," Kelly said. "I couldn't call him, otherwise."

"Maybe he doesn't care."

"What the hell do you mean?"

"Suppose it's just a business thing. Suppose she wasn't lying when she said he's just some dick she hired to find her brother. So it's not like he's Prince Charming, come in riding to the rescue."

"What, you figure he'd just cut her loose?"

Strauss shrugged. "I would."

"No, wait a sec. Why's he been tearing up the landscape, then? And who's this other prick she's claiming not to know?"

"First thing." Strauss raised a hand and started counting on his fingers. "Guy's pissed off because O'Malley tried to take him out. He goes for payback."

"A private dick fights back like this?"

"They're all ex-military these days, in security," Strauss said. "Titan, Blackwater, DynCorp, KBR, whoever. Paramilitaries. Private armies."

"How's this chick afford something like that?" Kelly asked. "Now you're talking outfits that do business with the Pentagon."

"So, something smaller. Or she made it worth this one guy's time, up to a point, and when O'Malley tried to cap him, he decided, why not stick around awhile? Get even? Call a bud to help him out."

"But if he doesn't care what happens to the girl…"

"He'll just keep kicking Gallo's ass around the block, until somebody puts him down."

"Could work to our advantage," Strauss suggested.

"If we brought them in."

"Dead or alive."

"I vote for dead."

"No fuss, no muss. No telling tales, that way. Nothing blows back on us."

"The brass is grateful, and we do a solid for the Family."

"Win-win," Strauss said, smiling.

"That just leaves the girl," Kelly said.

"What girl?"

"Right. But she was there, at headquarters. Seen talking to us."

"So? She came to ask about her brother, and we told her there was nothing she could do to help us find him. How're we suppose to know what happened to her, after that? As far as we know, she went home."

"And when it turns out that she never made her flight…?"

Strauss shrugged. "We open up another missing person file. Two Dirkses for the price of one."

"Maybe she found her bro and took him with her," Kelly said.

"Could happen. Anyway, both cases will be cold before you know it."

"Still, we shouldn't be too hasty, getting rid of her. Joe Borgio wants her kept safe."

That made his partner smile. "Sure. Hang on to her a few days. Break her in just a little."

"I was thinking keep her handy, if the dick changes his mind and calls back asking for a proof of life."

"Or that," Strauss said.

"Still haven't worked out how we bag them, though," Kelly said, "if they won't deal for the girl."

"If worse comes to worst," Strauss said, "we don't."

"We don't?"

"Go through the motions. Cover all the bases. Put the effort out there, Leo. How can Vinnie blame us when he's got an army on the street, and they get nowhere? Hell, there's just the two of us."

"He may not see it that way."

"So, we reason with him. Bring him around."

"You understand I'm talking about Vinnie Gallo, right?"

Strauss nodded. "He's just a man, Leo. It's not like he's bulletproof."

Market Street, Polonia, East Buffalo

IT WAS A GAMBLE, going back to Eddie Reems. Illicit arms dealers inevitably had connections to the underworld. There was a chance that Reems had done his basic math, put two and two together, coming up with a potential jackpot if he tipped the Gallo Family to Bolan's recent visit. Granted, Reems possessed no solid intel, couldn't tell the Mob where Bolan was, or offer anything beyond a physical description, and they'd have that anyway, from the *amici* he'd left breathing as his messengers.

There was a chance the Mob would have surveillance on the pawnshop, hoping that their target would run low on ammunition or require new hardware—as, in fact, he did. If that turned out to be the case, if they were drawn into a trap…well, then, they'd have to fight their way back out again.

Or go down trying, right.

From what he'd seen in Reems's arsenal, last time around, Bolan had made a shopping list. The mission had expanded from a hasty hit-and-git to something else entirely, and he needed the proper tools to carry out the job.

Reems looked surprised to see him, studied Johnny's face for future reference while he was shaking their hands and readily agreed that he could fill their needs if they had cash to spend. Thanks to the loans operations across the border, two of them with empty safes now, that was not a problem.

After Reems had put up his Closed sign and walked them to the backroom arsenal, it was a simple task to make the various selections Bolan had in mind. They'd be most vulnerable when they walked their acquisitions to the Mercury, prepared to leave the neighborhood, but since no trap had closed around them yet—and Bolan wouldn't let Reems touch a telephone until they hit the street—he thought they had a fairly decent chance of getting clear.

This time around, he bagged a Milkor MGL 6-shot grenade launcher in 40 mm, with a mix of high-explosive, pyrotechnic and antipersonnel rounds. For long-distance work, he added a Barrett XM500 chambered for .50 Browning Machine Gun rounds, with a striking range of some 2,500 yards. Scoring at that range came down to optics, in this case the rifle's AN/PVS-10 day/night scope. To back up Johnny's Glock, they took a Steyr AUG assault rifle, then doubled down on extra magazines and ammunition for their weapons, all around.

Reems named a price and flashed his dentures ear-to-ear as Bolan handed over banded blocks of cash. "Looks like you broke the bank," he commented.

"A couple of them," Bolan said, seeing no reason to be coy.

"And you're not finished yet, I take it, if you'll pardon my impertinence."

"Look on the bright side," Bolan told him. "Could be great for business."

"I prefer to be impartial in such matters," Reems explained. "Conflicts of interest are…unfortunate."

"And dangerous," Johnny added.

"As I'm very well aware," the dealer said. "Which is the very reason I avoid prying into the lives and business concerns of valued customers."

"But if you were asked," Bolan said, "you might let something slip."

Now Reems looked glum. "It's always possible," he granted.

"You could always say Joe Dirks stopped by," Bolan said. "And he's hoping to be reunited with his sister soon."

"His sister?"

"If she's still alive and well, that is."

"Of course."

"But failing that, it could be bad news for the family."

"The worst," Johnny added.

"I'll be sure to pass that on," Reems said. "If anybody asks."

Justice Building, Washington, D.C.

THE TELEVISION IN Hal Brognola's office was tuned to Headline News on CNN, as usual. Okay, sometimes he switched to Fox, but only for a laugh or to amaze himself at what some talking heads would say, straight-faced, if they were paid enough. This day was straight news, though. The big Fed glanced up from paperwork each time New York was mentioned, hoping there would be some bulletins from Buffalo.

So far, no luck.

He understood priorities, of course. When people lived in a world on fire, with wars and random acts of terrorism, demonstrations in the streets, whole national economies dangling by the seemingly thinnest of threads, there wasn't lots of on-air time available for relatively bush-league mafiosi dying on the U.S.–Canadian border.

Not yet.

But Brognola had been around enough Bolan campaigns to know that things were heating up, and rapidly. Before much longer, possibly by quitting time that afternoon, the story would be going national. Or was that "viral"? If some passerby produced a cell-phone video, uploaded it to YouTube or whatever, they could all be in the soup.

Deniability was paramount—and hell, this mission hadn't even been assigned from Stony Man—but in the current age, when everyone saw everything and knew it all, even when most of "it" was wrong, even an outright lie, security could take a major hit.

Brognola had been ruminating over steps that he might take to help the situation. Calling Bolan off wasn't an option; it never had been, in the time he'd known the big guy. Pitching in to help with extra hands—someone from Able Team, perhaps—would likely make things worse instead of better. He'd already spoken to the FBI, but Jerrod Hansen wasn't breaking any land-speed records, getting back to the big Fed with information from the Bureau's files on dirty cops in Buffalo.

So…what?

The good news was that very few people alive knew Bolan had survived the death scene Brognola had helped him stage in New York City's Central Park. Fewer still could pick the reborn warrior's face out of a lineup. Brognola and Stony Man were answerable only to the White House, but the fellow in the Oval Office didn't know that many of his covert orders were relayed to Mack Samuel Bolan.

Hal's phone rang, private line. The big Fed picked it up. "Brognola."

"Hansen. I've got something for you."

"Shoot."

"Two names. Detectives in the Buffalo PD, under continuing investigation for alleged association with the Gallo Family."

"I'm all ears."

"Leonard James Kelly. Michael Gunther Strauss."

"Gunther?"

"Likely a hand-me-down. There was a third stooge, Gregory Francis O'Malley, but he bought the farm a couple days ago. You might've heard about it, since the PD's caught your interest."

"It rings a bell," Brognola granted.

"Well, that's my bit," Hansen said. "You want to tell me anything?"

"It would be premature. Counterproductive, as we say."

"Yeah, yeah. You know my shop's not big on give and take, much less just giving."

"Great for karma, though," Brognola said.

"If I was Buddhist, sure."

"You could convert."

The G-man let that pass and said, "I notice some of Gallo's men are checking out these days."

"Does that bother you?" Brognola inquired.

"Not really. But…"

"If I need to ask you something else—"

"Don't even think about it," Hansen said, "unless you're ready to come clean."

"Nothing to tell," Brognola said.

"Your call." The line went dead.

A bridge burned, or a momentary tiff? Brognola shrugged it off, deciding he would worry about Hansen later.

After Buffalo.

Black Rock, Buffalo, New York

POLE CATS, ANOTHER strip club operated by the Gallo Family, occupied a half block of East Street, south of Buffalo's Religious Art Center. That site—the museum, not the bar—was formerly St. Francis Xavier Church, now a substantial tourist draw that also, unlike Pole Cats, offered wedding ceremonies for the well-to-do. Of course, a guy who drank enough at Pole Cats might start to believe that he was on his honeymoon, and there were ladies in the joint who would support that sensual illusion for a price.

The bar was open, music pulsing through its cinder block

walls, as Bolan and Johnny approached on foot. "Five dollar cover charge," Johnny observed.

"We'll talk them out of it," Bolan said.

"Hate to cheat the girls, though."

"They'll get over it."

The place was dark as soon as they walked in, with DayGlo paint daubed over black walls in a crazy-quilt design suggesting that the artist had been eight miles high or physically impaired. Behind a counter, mounted on a bar stool, sat a beefy fellow in a leather jacket, white T-shirt beneath it, with a thick gold chain around his neck.

"Five bucks apiece," he said.

"It's on the house," Bolan replied.

"Says who?"

The bouncer's eyes crossed as he focused on the Milkor's 40 mm muzzle, inches from his face.

"You lead the way," Bolan suggested.

"Sure, man. Don't get nervous with that thing."

The doorman led them through a curtain, music blaring now, two dancers intertwined and doing something kinky on a small stage at the far end of the room. More power to them, Bolan thought, and fired a round into the ceiling, angling to his right so the debris would fall behind the bar. The music kept playing, but he saw the dancers bolt offstage, and a couple dozen customers lunge for lit exits on unsteady legs. Most of them were half in the bag, or encumbered by erections that were wilting in the face of firepower.

Bolan lobbed his next round at a giant amplifier near the stage, unleashing a shower of sparks. The music didn't die, exactly, but the volume dropped by half, maybe two-thirds, the speakers that remained producing tinny sound with scratchy reverb grating on the ears. The doorman, on his knees now, hands raised overhead, was pleading, "Yo, man! Take it easy, will ya?"

"I'm looking for the manager," Bolan said.

"Right here, slick!" a voice called from the general direction of the stage, and then a wiry-looking guy was rapid-firing a small, shiny revolver, jerking it, forgetting that he ought to aim.

Johnny gave him a short burst from the Steyr AUG and dropped him in a twitching heap. The nickel-plated wheel gun spun away, grating across the floor to stop a few yards short of Bolan's feet. There went their access to the strip club's safe, but the soldier didn't mind. Torching the joint would do as well as robbing it.

"So, you're the messenger," he told the kneeling doorman.

"Huh?"

"Go back to Vinnie Gallo. Tell him this was courtesy of Zoe Dirks. You got it?"

"Who the fu—"

"Repeat it!"

"Courtesy of Zoe Dirks! Okay?"

"If his people damage her in any way, it just gets worse."

"Gets worse. I got it, man!"

"Then split."

"Funny," Johnny said, watching Bolan feed a pyrotechnic round into the Milkor's chamber.

"What is?" Bolan asked.

"The music they were playing when we came in."

"Sorry. Didn't notice."

"Talking Heads," Johnny said. "'Burning Down the House.'"

Buffalo Police Headquarters

SERGEANT MAHAN SHOVED a second stick of Nicorette into his mouth and muttered to himself, "This is getting out of hand."

The latest call was more bad news, another one of Vinnie Gallo's T&A bars up in smoke, and while that didn't bother Mahan much, it was a poor reflection on the force. More to the point, he was afraid they hadn't seen the end of it, that things were only on their way to getting worse.

So far, aside from Greg O'Malley, only hoodlums had been killed or injured. Some—including Rudy Mahan—might've said O'Malley brought it on himself, but that was just between themselves, behind the Blue Wall, not for public consumption. Officially, whatever came out on the tube or in the newspapers, there was a cop-killer at large, and every officer in Buffalo was totally committed to the manhunt.

If they weren't distracted by the escalating "gang war," right.

But Mahan didn't think it *was* a gang war. That required two gangs, and nothing he'd picked up so far suggested any other outfit moving on the Gallo Family.

What, then?

A rapping on his open door distracted Mahan. Turning from the paperwork in front of him, he saw Detective Eugene Franks.

"Got a second, Sarge?" Franks asked him.

"Just about."

"I'm trying to find Strauss or Kelly. Any idea where they are?"

"I couldn't say, offhand. What's up?"

"Well…"

"Spit it out."

"Joe Dirks," Franks said.

"Am I supposed to know him?"

"Nope. One of my missing persons."

"So?"

"So, I've been talking to his sister, out in California. Me and Greg O'Malley, switching off, whoever was around. And now, the Charleston House downtown is calling me to say *she*'s missing."

"Downtown? In *Buffalo?*"

"A few blocks over, yeah."

"When you say missing…"

"She didn't check out. All her stuff's still in the room, her purse included."

"Huh."

"I didn't know that she was flying out," Franks said. "Seemed like she would of tried to get in touch with me, so…"

"What?"

"I asked down at the desk, and she *was* here. Came asking for O'Malley. Flannery passed her to Strauss, since I was in the field."

"You going over there? The Charleston?"

"Thought I might as well."

"You'll keep me posted, eh?"

"Sure thing, Sarge."

"If I hear from Strauss or Kelly in the meantime," Mahan said, "I'll have them call you."

"Okay, then."

Franks left Mahan with something new to think about, and the beginnings of a sour feeling in his gut. O'Malley had been tight with Strauss and Kelly. Nothing odd about that, in the closed society of Buffalo PD, but there'd been times when Mahan thought that he was closer to the pair than to his partner. Nothing to support it, really. Just a feeling, but he'd learned to trust that kind of hunch, dealing with skells.

And Greg O'Malley had turned out to be a skell, himself.

A dead skell, now. But what about his buddy boys?

Something to ponder, when he had a minute. When the city wasn't burning down.

North Forest Acres, Buffalo

"WHOSE BRIGHT IDEA was it to snatch this broad?" Gallo inquired. His scowl seemed set in stone.

"The dicks did that," Joe Borgio answered. "Strauss and Kelly."

"I didn't ask who *did* it, Joe. I asked you whose *idea* it was."

"Theirs, Vin. She walked into the cop shop, asking them about her brother, and I guess they thought…why not? A way to shut her up,"

"That's one thing, if they'd iced her," Gallo said. "But, no. They call one of the guys who's running all around, kicking our ass on both sides of the border, and they *tease* him with it. Have I got that right?"

"The thinking was, he might come in to save her. Make some kind of deal."

"And how's that working?"

"Not so good, Vin."

"Not so freaking good at all. We're still getting our asses kicked by…what? Two guys? Cops can't find them. My soldiers sure as hell can't find them. What am I supposed to do now, Joe? You got another bright idea, or what?"

Borgio was about to answer when the phone on Gallo's desk rang. Line two blinking red at him. The number he shared only with Borgio, his *consiglieri* and the capos of the other Families. Calling to gloat, he thought, and picked it up.

"Hullo?"

"Hey, Vinnie," said a male voice that he didn't recognize. "You happy with the way your life's been going lately?"

"Who's this?" Gallo, being cautious, swallowed his anger.

"A friend of Zoe Dirks," the caller said. "Taking her brother out was bad enough, but now you've stuck your dick right in the ringer, Vin."

"Is that a fact?"

"You betcha." In the background, Gallo thought he heard a second voice say something about range and elevation. That made no sense.

"I tell you what," Gallo said. "If you wanna meet me like a man and do this thing, just pick a time and place. We'll see how it shakes out."

"Sounds like a plan," the stranger said. "But I'm not finished playing with you yet."

"What the hell is that supposed to—"

When the window in the east wall blew, it sprayed Gallo's study with bright, razor-edged shards of glass. He heard the slug punch through the west wall of the room as he was pitching headlong to the floor, dropping the phone, hoping the desk would cover him enough to save his life.

Meanwhile, the shots kept coming, ripping photographs and paintings off the walls, pounding his desk with sledgehammer strokes, and he could hear the echo of the gunfire rolling in behind the bullets, playing catch-up. It sounded as if someone was firing a .44 Magnum pistol inside an oil drum, louder than any shots Gallo had heard since he'd watched *Saving Private Ryan* in his basement theater and turned the volume up to critical, loving the carnage on the screen.

It wasn't quite so entertaining, now.

And then, as quickly as it had begun, the shooting stopped. Fearing a trick, Gallo remained huddled beneath his desk and called out to his underboss. "Hey, Joe! You dead?"

"Guess not," Borgio replied, after a long five seconds. "You?"

"I'm talking, aren't I?"

Gallo's housemen were arriving now, weapons in hand, too late. They clamored for a target.

"Well, he isn't in here!" Gallo snapped. "Check the grounds, for Christ's sake, will ya? If he slipped by one of you, I'm gonna have somebody's balls."

"Dumb idiot missed us both," Borgio said, as he lumbered to his feet.

"You think so?" Gallo asked him.

"Hey, we're standing here."

"That's the way he planned it. Bastard said he wasn't finished playing with me yet," Gallo explained. "I think it's time we taught his ass a whole new game."

8

Buffalo Niagara International Airport

The last thing Borgio wanted, at the moment, was to be a moving target on the streets of Buffalo. Given a choice, he would have found a panic room or bomb shelter somewhere and locked himself inside until the whole damned storm blew over.

But the trouble was, he *didn't* have a choice.

The meeting with a top lieutenant from the powerful Juárez Cartel had been arranged before this Dirks shit hit the fan, and neither Borgio nor his boss had thought to call it off when bodies started dropping around Buffalo. One thing: it flat-out slipped his mind. Another thing: who knew that it could get this bad in just a day and change.

Now, one Jesús Fernández was a quarter hour out from landing, and he'd be expecting the red carpet treatment from his hosts. That meant a hasty cleanup at the boss's house, so nobody could tell it had been shot to hell, and plenty of security around the visitors to make damn sure they didn't get a hangnail, much less have their brains blown out.

Juárez could sell them coke, meth, heroin, whatever, but they took their insults *very* personally. Fifty thousand dead and counting down below the border, in their never-ending drug wars, and the toll included judges, prosecutors, cops, archbishops, presidential candidate—you name it. Heads cut off and left on doorsteps, mass graves in the desert, families gunned down at funerals.

So, everything about the visit had to run like clockwork, even if the clock seemed to be busted at the moment. Any slipups could make matters so much worse that Borgio didn't even want to think about it.

Not that he could help but think, regardless.

He had brought eight soldiers with him to the airport, hoping it would be enough, guessing Fernández would have brought his own security along, as well. The private jet was an Embraer Legacy 600, retailing around $28 million, which Borgio guessed the cartel earned on any given day between their lunch break and siesta time. It needed a three-man crew and seated thirteen passengers. Joe Borgio stood beside his limo, two more waiting in the lineup, watching as the Mexicans deplaned. He counted ten and recognized Fernández in the middle of the pack, from photographs he'd seen.

The rest was basic protocol, Borgio approaching, offering his hand, while soldiers on both sides faced off and did the mandatory glaring thing. *Machismo* meant the same thing in Italian as it did in Spanish, weighed as heavily on any mafioso as it did on warlords from Juárez.

"Good flight?" Borgio inquired.

"Long flight," Fernández said. "I also had to make sure that our papers were in order."

Meaning bogus, since Fernández was a fugitive under indictment in the States, thumbing his nose at Uncle Sam by dropping in to deal with Vinnie Gallo personally. You could call that courtesy or showing off. Right now, it meant they shouldn't stand around the tarmac making chitchat, when they could be on the road.

"You wanna ride with me, or…?" Borgio asked, giving him the choice. He didn't care one way or another, since the limousines were bugged to pick up every word Fernández spoke between the airport and delivery to Gallo's doorstep.

"Why not?" the Mexican replied. "Enrique and José, with me. The rest of you, ride with these other *caballeros,* eh?"

They piled into the cars, and in another minute they were rolling. Borgio felt better, then, the simple act of movement soothing him. They cleared the airport, rolling north along Cayuga Road with three limos in line. They'd gone a mile or so when Borgio's driver said, "Hey, Boss, I think we got a tail."

Staying calm, he said, "So, shake it. And get on the horn, there. Have the fellas in the other cars ready to take them out."

"THEY'VE SPOTTED US," Johnny announced. "I'm making my move."

Bolan was ready in the backseat, where he had more combat stretch than riding shotgun, as the Mercury surged forward, its six-speed automatic transmission shifting smoothly under urging from its 3.0-liter Duratec 30 V6. The limousines would have more power underneath their hoods, but they were also vastly larger, heavier and loaded down with men.

Armed men.

Bolan was ready on his left as they began to pass the last limo in line, its blacked-out windows gliding down to grant a view of swarthy, snarling faces. Someone raised a pistol, but never got the chance to aim, as Bolan squeezed off two rounds from his Milkor MGL. His weapon might resemble an old-fashioned tommy gun on steroids, but it operated like a double-action revolver, its smooth action nearly impossible to jam—and there was no jam this time, as he blazed away.

Round one was buckshot, twenty-seven metal pellets weighing just under one ounce apiece, ripping through faces, skulls, torsos—whatever might be in their way. Round two was thermobaric, containing duel explosive charges. The first charge burst the grenade's casing and sprayed a cloud of inflammable fuel that mixed with atmospheric oxygen. The second charge then created a massive blast wave significantly longer in duration than any produced by condensed explosives.

Result, in this case: a mini-firestorm on wheels, explosions and the roar of flames consuming flesh and screams.

"One down," Bolan said, but his brother didn't need to hear it. Johnny was already powering the vehicle toward target number two.

No problem killing these guys, either, since they knew the

man they wanted was a passenger inside the lead car. Taking out as many of his soldiers as they could was mandatory, as a setup for the final act.

The soldiers riding within the second limo had observed the fiery end of their associates and obviously didn't want to share it. Bolan couldn't blame them, but he felt no trace of sympathy for anyone who served the Gallo Family or the Juárez Cartel. He owed Brognola big-time for the tip that Jesús Fernández would be flying into Buffalo today, the more so since, by rights, the big Fed should have given that information to the DEA. The end result might satisfy headquarters, but if they had known about Brognola's lapse, the brass would still be pissed.

Too bad.

The second limo had begun evasive action, swerving back and forth across two lanes, with shooters peering out the windows, aching for a chance to take their shot. Johnny slid over to the right and cleared the field for Bolan to deliver an HE round, punching through the limo's trunk lid, detonating there and taking out the rear axle assembly, just before the fuel tank blew.

Two down.

There might have been survivors in the wreckage, but they weren't his problem any longer. It had turned into a race now, and the Executioner couldn't simply blow the last limo apart or toast its occupants with thermobaric rounds. He needed one of them alive.

But only one.

Gaining on their quarry, Johnny veered off to the left, giving Bolan access to the fleeing limo's left rear tire. His buckshot round reduced the steel-belt radial to so much flapping tissue paper, and the driver started losing it. His tank was all over the road as Johnny pulled alongside, putting Bolan's open window level with the driver's door.

Another buckshot round took out the driver's window and the man behind it, killing him and anyone who might have occupied the shotgun seat. That was the end of any steering for the limo, as it slewed away from Bolan's ride and tried to climb a guardrail on the east side of the northbound highway.

Johnny hit the brakes, and both of them were EVA in seconds flat, circling the limousine and pulling open doors. A few short bursts from Bolan's Spectre and his brother's Steyr AUG eliminated any vestige of resistance, and they dragged the sole survivor out into the light, hauling him swiftly toward the waiting Mercury Milan.

North Forest Acres, Buffalo

VINNIE GALLO WASN'T normally the nervous type, but since he'd been taking hits from Buffalo to Niagara Falls and back again, he felt an edginess that couldn't be denied. It was bad luck, the Mexicans arriving in the midst of all his other trouble—bad luck and bad planning, if he told the absolute unvarnished truth—but there was nothing he could do about it.

Now, on top of all the rest, their inconvenient guests were late.

Not late arriving at the airport, mind you. He'd received Joe Borgio's call announcing their arrival, right on time. In fact, the limos had been rolling when he spoke to Joe, an easy run from the airport in Cheektowaga, Buffalo's second-largest suburb, to Borgio's doorstep, if they didn't dick around.

So where in hell *were* they?

He looked around his office, scowling. The windows were boarded over, waiting for the glazier to arrive with special armored glass, but at the moment Gallo liked the plywood better. No one could see through it, putting crosshairs on his forehead. When he met the Mexicans, they wouldn't be in here, would never guess some prick had come along and shot the hell out of his private office, in his own damned house.

The phone rang, nearly making him jump and spill his sixteen-year-old Bushmills single malt. He covered that by firing off a string of curses, finishing before he answered, midway through the second ring.

"Hullo?"

"Hey, Vinnie. How's it hanging?"

And he would have known that damned voice anywhere. "Listen, you piece of—"

"No, *you* listen, Vinnie."

Then the voice was gone, another coming on the line. "Hey, Vin? I'm sorry, man."

Joe Borgio.

"Joe? What the hell is this? Where are you? What happened to the—"

"Visitors from Juárez?" Now the first guy was back, taunting him. "They won't be coming, Vinnie."

"What the hell do you mean, they won't be coming?" But he knew already, guessed that he would hear about it on his TV in a little while, maybe a special bulletin to interrupt whatever crappy show was rotting brains today.

But just in case he didn't get it, Mr. Smartass spelled it out. "They're dead, Vin. Gone to cartel purgatory."

"What's the deal with Joe?" Gallo asked, feeling just a little dead himself, inside.

"Depends. You want him back?"

"What do you think?"

"I'm asking you."

"Hell, yes. I want him back, goddamn it!"

"Then," the caller said, "I guess it's time we made a deal."

East Side, Buffalo, New York

KELLY WAS READY when his cell phone rang again, thinking the jerk-off who'd hung up on him had tried to run some kind of game, see if he'd sweat a little. The bastard didn't know who he was dealing with, but he was going to find out.

"Hallo." Keeping it neutral for the moment, just in case it was someone from headquarters.

"What the fuck do you think you're doing?" Vinnie Gallo demanded.

"Hey, Mr. G." He saw his partner's ears perk up at that,

the corners of his mouth turn down. "I don't know what you mean."

"Bullshit! You pissed somebody off big-time, *Detective*. He's been calling me. He paid a freaking visit to *my house!* The place is shot to hell! You gonna make believe you don't know what that's all about?"

"Hold on. We thought—"

"Right there's your first mistake," Gallo said, interrupting him. "A button man doesn't think. He just does what he's told."

"We had to grab—"

"*Shut up!* You're gonna give confession on a goddamn cell phone, now? What are you, high or stupid? Did they teach you anything at the academy besides ten ways to rub your nightstick?"

Kelly's cheeks were flaming. He felt dizzy from the clashing anger and humiliation, grateful that he had been seated when he took the call.

"I'm trying to explain why—"

"Don't explain it. *Fix it!*"

"Okay, sure. Just tell me what you want."

"You're gonna hand the package off to some of my boys. Meet them at Riccardo's, around the back door. Half an hour."

"But Riccardo's is way over—"

"So, use your freaking siren! If you're late, don't bother coming. Just start looking for a place to hide."

"Okay. We'll be there."

"And the package better not be damaged, understand me?"

"Well, we had to use a Tase—"

"Aside from normal wear and tear. None of your shadow's kinky stuff."

"Mick never—"

"Safe and sound. I've got to trade it off for something I've lost, now. If the swap falls through, you might consider moving to a desert island. Buy yourself a little time."

"Again, I wanna say—"

"Blah-blah, same bull, yada-yada. Make the drop, then

light a candle for yourself. If something goes wrong, you're Sunday's turkey dinner."

"Right. Mr. G—"

And the line went dead.

"The guy sounds pissed," Strauss said, not half as worried-looking as he should have been.

"Ya think?"

"What's going on?"

"He needs to swap the girl for something, someone, I don't know. We drop her at Riccardo's. Half an hour."

"Half an hour? Christ, it's all the way—"

"Don't tell me where it is! Just get her out here!"

"Easy, partner."

"Every minute we spend talking is a minute off our lives. You get it?"

"Yeah, yeah." Strauss was on his feet and moving now.

"Hey, Mick."

"Yeah."

"Tell me that you didn't mess around with her."

"Okay."

"Because he said if you did anything—"

"Hey, Leo. We agreed. I may've felt her up a little, to get her motor revving. Nothing, really."

"Jesus wept."

"The hell with her. She's nothing but a—"

Kelly vaulted to his feet, crossed the room in three long strides, Glock in his hand before he was aware of drawing it. He jammed it underneath his partner's chin and forced his head back, seeing fear in Strauss's eyes at last.

"Listen to me, asshole. If I have to die because you couldn't keep it in your pants, I'm gonna hang on long enough to blow your rotten brain out of your head. Hear me?"

"I hope your finger isn't on that trigger, partner."

"Go. And. Get. The. Girl."

ZOE DIRKS COULD hear her captors arguing, and while she couldn't make out much of what they actually said, she knew that strife between them would rebound on her in ways she didn't want to think about. Kelly, the cooler-headed of the two so-called detectives, obviously didn't care for having her around, but Zoe knew he couldn't simply let her go, to testify against his partner and himself. He might as well surrender now and book a reservation at the nearest penitentiary.

Kelly was fully capable of killing her, she thought—as she believed he might have killed her brother, or at least participated in the cover-up that followed.

Still, it was the other one, Mick Strauss, who frightened her the most. She dreaded being left along with him, still felt his hands crawling across her body like two big, repulsive spiders as he'd "frisked" her, smirking that he had to check for weapons or to see if she was "wired." It may have been the longest frisk in history, and it had left her feeling soiled, unclean.

Better a bullet in the head, she thought, than to be mauled and violated by that animal.

Of course, that wouldn't be her choice. It might be both.

She had considered praying, a reflex from childhood Sunday school, but couldn't think of any time when she'd been helped by invisible friends in the sky. Zoe had reached a point where every breath felt precious to her, and she didn't want to waste them groveling to someone or something that never deigned to answer.

When they came after her, she had decided to resist. It would be futile, but at least she wouldn't die feeling disgusted with herself for doing nothing. She could kick, bite, scratch, perhaps succeed in marking one or both of them to the extent that it aroused suspicion. With the state of modern forensic science, who could say that a flake of her dandruff, a drop of saliva or blood, might not remain to hang them, somewhere down the road.

No hanging in New York, she thought. In fact, she wasn't sure if anybody had been executed in the state during her lifetime. Make it life in prison, then—which, to her mind, was even worse. It nearly made her smile to think about two bastard crooked cops caged up with men they'd put away.

Nearly.

The argument in the other room was winding down. Zoe sat upright on the twin bed she had been allotted, facing the door. She listened, heard heavy footsteps approaching over cheap linoleum, and braced herself for anything. If this was it, the end of life, at least she wouldn't go out whimpering.

The door opened. Her heart skipped and her stomach rolled when she saw that it was Strauss, with no sign of Kelly in the background to restrain him.

"What?" She hooked her fingers into claws, prepared to spring if he approached her.

"Come on, babe," he said. "We're going for a little ride."

Niagara Falls State Park

THERE WAS NO HAPPY medium in choosing sites for the exchange. The falls were public property—the oldest state park in America, if Bolan could trust his guidebook—featuring the three world-famous waterfalls, Cave of the Winds and a monument to legendary electrical engineer Nikola Tesla, among other attractions. Millions of tourists visited the park each year, and while he hated putting any innocent civilians in the line of fire, Bolan was hoping that their presence, with the normal complement of law enforcement found in any crowded public place these days, would keep the opposition honest.

To a point, at least.

He'd worked out details of the trade with Johnny, before pitching it to Gallo on the phone. He'd considered Goat Island, but knew police or mafiosi could seal off the place by commanding three bridges. Instead, they had decided to swap prisoners at the Niagara Adventure Theater, off Robert Moses Parkway. It was an IMAX theater, running hourly presentations of *Niagara: Legends of Adventure* on a forty-five-foot screen, submerging viewers with Dolby Digital surround sound technology. Members of the audience would be oblivious to anything beyond the theater's four walls.

When the time came, in the middle of a screening, Johnny

would be walking Borgio to meet the hoods who'd be escorting Zoe Dirks. If all went well, they'd come together in the parking lot, make the exchange, and walk away to their separate vehicles without disturbing any passersby.

But if anything went wrong...

The theater stood in the midst of lushly wooded grounds with plenty of places for a sniper to conceal himself. The Barrett's range and optics meant that Bolan didn't have to be on top of any action going down outside the IMAX hall. He needed only line of sight, with nothing to obstruct a bullet traveling in excess of three thousand feet per second, striking with some thirteen thousand foot-pounds of destructive energy.

The Barrett's detachable box magazine held ten .50-caliber rounds, and he had a dozen spare mags in reserve. He could switch out in seconds, if it was required, and empty a magazine as quickly as he acquired targets. Bottom line, if he could see it, he could kill it—though eliminating moving targets still required a specialist's skill.

"You think they'll even bring her?" Johnny asked, as they were rolling west on Robert Moses. Borgio was riding in the trunk, handcuffed and gagged.

"They will," Bolan confirmed. "I made it clear to Gallo that we won't deliver Joe without a clear view of the girl, alive and well."

"I wouldn't count on *well*," Johnny said.

"We dictated terms. If it turns out that Gallo violated them, he pays the price."

"And if he didn't?"

"Oh, he still pays. But you have your client back."

"And out of here, ASAP."

They'd picked Chautauqua County–Jamestown Airport, fifty-seven miles from Buffalo, a small but serviceable facility with a pilot standing by. He would take Zoe to Detroit, and she could make her own way home from there, talk to the FBI or anybody else that caught her fancy if she wanted to break silence, but Bolan doubted that she'd try to make things tough on Johnny.

That was, if they got her out alive.

If it went down the other way, a double-cross at the last minute, Bolan thought they were prepared. Johnny would have the Steyr and his Glock, covered by Bolan with the .50-caliber Barrett. He couldn't use the Milkor MGL beyond four hundred yards, so Johnny would be taking it along as backup, in the Mercury, in case the hand-off went to hell.

And after, if they got the client out alive, with both of them intact—then what?

The war went on. What else?

It had already gone too far for compromise, and Johnny wasn't clear yet, for the cop-killing.

Whatever happened in the next few hours, the Executioner had work to do.

9

Niagara Falls State Park

"I can't believe Joe let himself get bagged like this," Richie Montana said, as they approached the drop.

"Don't worry about what Joe did or he didn't do," the crew boss, Danny Galleani, said. "Watch where you're driving, so we get there in one piece."

"We're there already," Richie answered back. "You're looking at the theater, right there."

"Weird freaking place to make the trade," said Mario Venturi, riding in the backseat with Zoe Dirks.

"You ever seen that movie they show here?" asked John Politi, who flanked their captive like a stocky bookend. "It's not bad."

"Same movie all the time?" Tony Frazetta asked him, from the nearest jump seat.

"It's Niagara Falls," Politi said. "You figure they should run some flick about the Amazon in Africa?"

Lou Stella, in the other jump seat, barked a laugh at that. "The Amazon's in Mexico, Einstein," he told Politi. "You oughta study your geography."

"Shut up about the friggin' Amazon, for Chrissakes!" Galleani snapped. "Did anybody see the others, coming in?"

No answer from his troops. He guessed their backup team was hidden pretty well, there in the woods around the theater. He hoped so, anyway. If he and his guys were out there on their own and anything went wrong, he didn't want to think about the repercussions.

Turkey time, for damn sure, if they lost the underboss.

The Lincoln MKT Town Car was rolling slowly to a halt, Montana braking on the outer limits of the spacious parking lot. "Gun check," Galleani said, reaching down between his feet to lift a Mini-Uzi submachine gun from the floorboards. Underneath his left arm, heavy in its holster, hung a Glock 37, the .45-caliber model.

All his men were double-packed, as well, each with a handgun plus a larger weapon, whether automatic or a scattergun. They didn't plan on fighting, if their little act played out the way it was supposed to, but the first thing Galleani had learned, when he was still a punk-ass juvie hanging on a street corner in Buffalo, was that whatever *could* go wrong in any given situation nearly always did.

His second lesson: if you had a couple guns to smooth things over, you were cool.

"Remember, now," he told the others. "We just trade the girl for Joe. The other team moves in to bag these humps, once we take care of business. Got it?"

Muttered affirmations came from the Lincoln's rear seat, but nothing from the girl. She couldn't say much with her mouth duct-taped, which was a bonus. She'd been weepy when they put her in the car, and Galleani hated all that pleading crap. Not that he wished her any harm, per se. She was a total stranger, and a righteous babe, but he had one job at the moment and he couldn't screw it up.

"All set?"

More muttering, but eager now. His crew liked action, which was good—as long as none of them provoked a shitstorm when they were supposed to simply make the trade and split. If somebody screwed up, then Galleani was prepared to cap the stupid prick himself.

It was late afternoon, with only a few tourists hanging around to catch the next show, which didn't start for half an hour. Their business should be finished by that time, Galleani figured. What happened to the bystanders was someone else's problem. If his luck held, he would be on his way back home to Buffalo, Joe Borgio fat and sassy in the backseat, well before the first caps started popping in the park.

"Let's go," he said, and stepped out of the car.

THE BACKUP SOLDIERS had begun arriving twenty minutes after Bolan was in place. They missed him in his tree, well camouflaged, and fanned out through the wooded acreage surrounding the Niagara Adventure Theater, laying their trap as Vincent Gallo had commanded. Some of them might be ex-military, he supposed, but Bolan understood the mindset well enough to know that there would be no cops among them. Sending out bent detectives to pull a solitary hit was one thing; fielding them for a pitched battle where they might be called on to face off against their fellow officers was something else entirely.

So as far as Bolan was concerned, the park had just become a free-fire zone.

He'd counted fifteen infiltrators and supposed that there might be another handful on the far side of the theater he couldn't see, barring the back door to escape after the prisoner exchange had been completed. Call it twenty, then—two Barrett magazines—besides whoever Gallo sent to make the swap itself. Bolan's problem wasn't killing them, but rather doing it with ample speed and accuracy to preserve his brother's life and that of Zoe Dirks.

The rest could go to hell.

The soldier had considered slipping out among the members of the ambush party, cutting throats or letting his Beretta whisper them to sleep forever, but he'd fought the impulse, staying where he was and sticking to the plan he'd hatched with Johnny. Any deviation from that scheme opened the door to unforeseen catastrophe. He owed it to his brother—and the woman he had never met—to play it straight, with a strategy that had the best chance of success.

Joe Borgio could live or die this day, for all he cared. At best, the underboss was already on borrowed time.

Bolan tracked the Lincoln through its long, cautious approach, its occupants concealed behind the deeply tinted windows. That was fine. He could have reached them with the Barrett, even if the vehicle had been advertised for sale as "bulletproof," but he didn't want a bloodbath in the crew wagon, with Zoe Dirks hemmed in by nervous guns. At least outside the car, she'd have a chance to run.

"They're here," he told the mouthpiece of his Bluetooth headset.

And his brother's voice replied, in Bolan's ear, "Okay."

"I've got an extra fifteen on the ground, my side," Bolan reported.

"Three back here, that I can see," Johnny replied.

His brother would likely have to deal with those himself, Bolan thought, if Gallo's drop team let him start back toward the Mercury. Three wasn't bad, if Johnny had them spotted. On the other hand, if they moved up, there was a chance Bolan could reap them with the Barrett from his sniper's aerie in the great elm tree.

Plenty of targets for the big gun, either way.

"They're in the lot," he said, keeping his voice low-pitched. "Slowing. Okay, they've stopped. You have seven civilians hanging out in front."

"No problem," Johnny answered, as if saying it would make it true.

The Lincoln's crew had no view of the Mercury from where they sat. It was a lonesome stroll of forty yards or so from their position to the theater, specifically the corner where his brother would emerge in moments, with Joe Borgio in tow. There was a chance, Bolan realized, that someone from the backup team would try for Johnny on that walk, but he guessed their orders were to see Borgio safely exchanged before they started anything.

Downrange, armed men began to climb out of the Lincoln.

Zoe Dirks was terrified. Who wouldn't be? When the perverted cop, Mick Strauss, had told her she was going home, the first thing that had flashed across her mind was *Soylent Green,* the sci-fi flick where "going home" meant dying to escape a hopeless world. She'd thought her kidnappers were taking her on what had once been called a one-way ride… but, no. They drove to a pizzeria, parked in back and then delivered her to gangsters who reminded her of apes dressed up for church.

Then, Zoe had been sure she was about to die. Presumably, the cops wanted to let somebody else handle the dirty work. Crammed into the Lincoln MKT Town Car with six gorillas, Zoe had found her life flashing before her eyes, extremely disappointing in its brevity and opportunities not taken, since she liked to play it safe.

How safe was *this?*

It took another little while for her to realize that they were actually going somewhere, not just looking for a place to dump her corpse. Nobody spoke to her, of course. In fact, they barely spoke at all, except for passing comments about people they called "Mr. Borgio" and "Mr. G." Something about a "drop" and "backup" that she didn't follow.

Now, after driving through some woods, they had arrived outside a building signs identified as the Niagara Adventure Theater. She pictured sitting through a movie with these goons and almost laughed behind her duct-tape gag, bursting the airy bubble of hysteria with will alone.

"Remember, now," their leader rumbled. "We just trade the girl for Mr. Borgio. The other team moves in to bag these humps, once we take care of business. Got it?"

Everybody seemed to understand.

"All set?" He paused again, then said, "Let's go."

They climbed out of the car on both sides, one of Zoe's backseat babysitters dragging her along behind him. They had left her hands free, but she didn't feel like fighting anymore. What was the point, with all those guns around her? And if they were serious about releasing her, why take a chance at blowing it?

Outside the Lincoln, still surrounded, Zoe noticed several tourists idling near the theater. A couple of them watched the new arrivals, blanching at the sight of guns in open view, and warning those around them in hushed tones. Within another minute, she imagined, someone would be on a cell phone, calling the police.

And what would happen to her then?

As if in answer to her silent thought, two men appeared, stepping around a corner of the theater. On cue, the leader of her escorts said, "That's them. C'mon."

Then they were moving, setting off across the parking lot, the two men from the corner headed their way. Zoe didn't recognize the shorter of the pair approaching them, hands clasped behind his back, but she knew Johnny Gray immediately. Somehow, it appeared, he had arranged for her release. By kidnapping a hostage of his own? The "Mr. Borgio" her hulking entourage was so concerned about?

And then she understood about *the other team,* waiting to *bag these humps.* One of the "humps" was Johnny, obviously. Zoe hadn't spilled his name to Strauss and Kelly, but she might as well have, since she'd drawn him straight into a trap.

Dizzy with fear and anger—mostly at herself—she rounded on the nearest gunman, clawing at his startled face.

JOHNNY SAW THE strike coming and couldn't believe it. They were so close, seemed to have a decent chance of making it, then Zoe spun and lashed out at the mafioso on her left, her nails raking bloody furrows down his cheek.

The guy growled, flinched from her and struck back in an instant, clubbing Zoe with the hand that clutched a sawed-off 12-gauge pump shotgun. Johnny was bringing up his autorifle when Joe Borgio barked out, "Fuck this!" and bolted for the nearest entrance to the theater.

And just like that, it went to hell.

Johnny shot Borgio on the run, one 5.56 mm NATO round

that drilled a pinhole in his back, left of the spine, then tumbled through his guts and blew out through his navel with a fist-size exit wound. The underboss let out a squeal, hit the pavement and began a crazy, broken crawl that looked like swimming, but the only liquid anywhere in sight was Borgio's own blood trail.

Forget him.

Johnny swiveled toward the escort team, in time to see one of them literally lose his head. It ruptured—make that *detonated*—like a melon with a cherry bomb inside, but without any sound of an explosion, just a huge wet *splat,* as blood and mangled brains flew everywhere. The echo of a gunshot came to Johnny's ears a second later, rolling toward the theater from somewhere in the woods beyond.

The Barrett, right.

Johnny was firing then, before his enemies recovered from the sight of Borgio going down and being sprayed with blood from one of their *fratelli.* With his AUG on semiauto, he put one round through the soldier who'd punched Zoe, spinning him around with the explosive force of impact, shotgun airborne as the big man fell.

Zoe was on the ground and bloody-faced, but there was no time to concern himself with that. Flesh wounds could be repaired; a bullet in the brainpan, not so much.

So, when he saw the shooter on her left level his Uzi at her kneeling figure, Johnny targeted him next. It was a hasty shot, center of mass, but did the trick, punching through the mafioso's rib cage on his right-hand side and spalling through lungs, heart and aorta. Dying on his feet, the shooter still managed to fire a short burst from his SMG, but it went over Zoe's head and gouged a line of divots in the asphalt yards beyond her.

Bolan's next round came in while Johnny was finishing his second man, another head shot, but a bit off-center. This one hit the tallest of the thugs still on their feet and sheared off roughly half his skull, on a diagonal from left eyebrow to right earlobe. Johnny could have sworn the one eye still remaining blinked at him before it rolled back, showing only white, and the machine-gunner collapsed.

And that left two.

"I'm on the short one."

With his brother's voice in his ear, Johnny pivoted to take the shooter farthest on his left, had a fleeting peripheral glimpse of the other guy's end, as a .50-caliber full-metal-jacket round burst through his chest in a bright crimson spray. Johnny's man had a vaguely stunned look on his face, his M4 carbine beginning to stutter as Johnny squeezed off two quick round of his own.

And before the guy fell, Johnny raced to Zoe, ignoring the duct tape and blood on her face, grabbing one of her arms and yanking her upright, a sob-gasp escaping from somewhere as she realized that she wasn't done yet.

"Focus now!" Johnny snapped at her, shoving her off toward his car. "Run like hell!"

THE FIRST SHOT from the theater had mobilized the backup team. Whatever signal they'd been waiting for went out the window with the crack of gunfire and the vision of Joe Borgio going down. They rushed the parking lot, moving en masse to help their point men handle Johnny and the girl, and weren't prepared for sudden thunder as the Barrett started hammering the soldiers from the Lincoln Town Car.

Any scheme they'd drawn up in advance began to fall apart then, as the best-laid plans are prone to do in battle. Combat was a fluid, living thing, where the reactions of an enemy could be surmised, but never quite predicted. A plan that worked on paper often fell apart when living people found themselves receiving fire and wound up fighting for their lives.

And so it was, this day. Bolan's first clap of thunder from the .50-caliber Barrett startled the nearest mafiosi, bringing eyes and guns around to seek the source of that explosive sound. One shot wasn't enough for them to peg him, and the next two came so quickly that the soldiers on the ground had no time to react effectively. But some of them were on him now, the others keeping after Johnny and the woman in their flight.

Eight rounds remained in the Barrett's magazine, since he had started out with ten, plus one in the firing chamber. Bolan swiveled on his perch, legs braced, both hands required to aim the thirty-pound XM500. He could probably have taken down his nearest targets without scoping them, but with the AN/PVS-10 they were larger than life, angry faces filling the eyepiece, exploding in Technicolor close-up when he stroked the rifle's trigger, slamming death downrange.

Of the fifteen he'd counted, six abandoned their original assignment to go after him. Two were fairly close and on his left, four scattered widely on his right. Bolan took the nearest of them first, squeezing off a round as soon as the telescope's reticle centered on-target, tracking from one skull's detonation to the next. It was the paradox of sniping: killing from a distance, when your mark seemed close enough for you to look him in the eye and watch his life go out, as if you were switching off a lamp.

Two down, and Bolan had to swivel through 110 degrees to bring the next mark under fire. By then, a couple of the four on his right side had seen their friends go down and were retreating through the woods, apparently deciding they would rather live to fight another day than face the Barrett's devastating fire.

Too late.

Bolan took down his third opponent with a shot high in the chest, the explosive impact flipping the guy over backward to drop him facedown on the grass. That convinced number four that he ought to be running for daylight, his mission forgotten, hell-bent on escape without firing a shot. Bolan lined up between his pumping shoulder blades, squeezed off his seventh round and blew the runner's heart out through his sternum.

Checking out the field, he saw the other nine torpedoes still pursuing Johnny and the girl. They'd started firing now, Johnny replying with his Steyr AUG to cover Zoe's getaway.

She was almost out of sight, nearing the southwest corner of the theater, but whether she'd be met by other guns was anybody's guess.

Bolan could only help with targets he could see.

Precision was the hallmark of a master sniper. Once a target was selected, hesitation lasted no longer than was required to frame the mark, steady the weapon and send death to keep its rendezvous with fragile flesh.

Leaving the runners on his right to find their own way from the woods, Bolan targeted the farthest soldier from his vantage point—the nearest to his brother—and sent forty-two grams of destruction hurtling toward impact at three thousand feet per second.

The mobster never knew what hit him. By the time the bloody remnant of his face slapped pavement, Bolan had already found another target and destroyed it. Chaos was in the ranks now, as the hunters realized that they were prey.

And there was nothing left for them to do but die.

JOHNNY DOUBLE-TAPPED the last punk who was still upright, and had turned to follow Zoe when he heard her squeal. It wasn't like a movie scream, but she had torn the duct tape from her mouth after she took that hard shot to the face, and she was in good voice.

Trouble.

He slid around the corner of the theater and saw three shooters facing Zoe, maybe thirty feet in front of him. They stood between her and the Mercury Milan, guns leveled from the hip. There'd be no getaway unless he took them out, and any one of them could make it pointless with a single shot at Zoe Dirks.

No time to waste.

"Zoe! Down!" he shouted, and cut loose with his Steyr AUG. A thumb-flick switched the piece from semi- to full-auto, and he held the trigger down, strafing his opponents with the remnants of his 30-round magazine. They skittered through a jerky death-dance, slipping in their own blood as it pattered down like rain, two of them managing to squeeze off wild shots even as they fell.

Zoe hit the deck, cringing, but she'd been fast enough to save herself. The shots fired by her would-be killers rippled overhead and chipped a zigzag pattern on the wall of the theater behind her. Johnny was beside her in another second, lifting her again and steering her around the corpses, toward their ride.

"They were… I thought… How did you…?"

"Get in the car," he said. "We'll talk about it later."

"But—"

"You're going home," he told her. "And I don't want any argument about it."

Zoe didn't argue. She didn't say another word, in fact, as Johnny put her in the Mercury's backseat.

"Stay down and out of sight," he ordered. "We've still got another stop to make."

Silence had fallen on the park, and it would likely be a few more minutes yet before the law arrived with sirens banshee-wailing. Johnny meant to be well clear by then, but first he had to find his brother.

They'd arranged two meeting points, the second as a backup if their plan unraveled. Johnny was supposed to get the hell away from there if his brother missed both connections, taking Zoe solo to the airport, but he wasn't sure that he could do that. Even though they seldom saw each other, trying to imagine life—the world—without his brother in it was an exercise that sickened him.

But his brother was there, a shadow breaking off from others in the parkland forest, hopping in as Johnny slowed the car, handing his rifle back to wide-eyed Zoe in the rear. She seemed about to say something, then evidently changed her mind and set the big gun down beside her feet.

"All good?" Johnny asked.

"So far," Bolan replied, checking his watch. "We've got a plane to catch."

10

North Forest Acres, Buffalo

"All dead?" The words tasted like ashes in the back of Vincent Gallo's throat.

"All but the two," his *consigliere* said. The look on Jerry Portoghesi's face was grim, going on ugly.

"Right. The two that ran away."

"To hear them tell it, there was nothing they could do. Joe took the first hit, and it fell apart from there."

"To hear *them* tell it," Gallo echoed. "I still got some questions for them, when they get here."

"Sure."

"What do the cops say?"

Portoghesi shrugged. "They're barely getting started. It's a madhouse over there, from what I hear."

"How many did we lose, again?"

The *consigliere* counted on his fingers, and finally told Gallo, "Twenty-three, with Joe."

"Goddamn it!"

"Something that I might suggest…"

"Spit it out."

"Bring reinforcements over from across the river," Portoghesi said. "Al took some hits, but no one's hassling him right now."

"That's good. I'll call him. What else?" Gallo asked.

"Well…I've been thinking that we haven't exactly got our money's worth from the city's finest."

"Kelly and Strauss."

Portoghesi nodded slowly. "Sure, they bagged the broad, but now that's backfired on us. They should make it right."

"And how would they do that?"

"Do their jobs. Work the street and squeeze their informants, whatever the hell they have to do. Get something on these hitters and pin them down."

The whole department was already working that side of the street, but what the hell. Gallo agreed with Portoghesi that the two limp dicks owed something to the Family, after the way they'd screwed the pooch.

"You call them, eh? I don't think I could stand to talk to them right now."

"No problem, Vin."

"And while you're doing that, I'll get Al moving on those soldiers. Should have twenty, twenty-five that he can spare, at least."

"They could be over here within the hour," Portoghesi said.

"All right, then. If you think of something else…"

"I'm on it, Vin."

Before he speed-dialed Cavallaro's number, Gallo poured himself a double shot of Bushmills single malt whiskey and threw it back in one gulp, shivering a little as the liquid heat rushed down his gullet, spreading out from there. He'd heard somewhere that alcohol was a depressant, wasn't sure exactly what that meant, and didn't care. He was depressed enough already, damn it, but the whiskey calmed him, helped him clarify his thoughts and focus on what still remained for him to do, if he was going to survive.

His Family was losing more than cash and soldiers in the shitstorm that had blown up out of nowhere, overnight. The greatest loss had been *prestige,* with damage done to Gallo's reputation that could be repaired only through swift, dynamic and decisive action. If he dicked around much longer, even if he wound up winning in the end, the Families that ran surrounding territories might decide that it was time to move on Buffalo. Hell, the Commission might sit down without him and elect someone to take his place.

He wouldn't leave without a fight, of course. Unless they hit him first. But fighting meant the final ruin of the Family he had inherited and worked his ass off to expand, growing more powerful and influential over time. Was he prepared to see it all go up in flames around him, just to prove he wasn't someone his so-called *fratelli* could step in and push aside?

Why not?

Say what you would about the brotherhood, *La Cosa Nostra,* he'd never known a boss who bowed out quietly or put his own head on the chopping block. Whatever any jealous, greedy bastards wanted from his Family, they'd have to come and take by force.

Beginning now.

Chautauqua County-Jamestown Airport,
Jamestown, New York

BOLAN'S CHOICE OF airports had two asphalt runways and was served by only one commercial carrier: United Express, with flights to Bradford, Pennsylvania, and Cleveland, Ohio. Nationally, it was ranked as a non-primary commercial service airport, meaning fewer than ten thousand takeoffs per year.

Which was perfect.

No one would be watching out for Zoe Dirks at such a small facility, so soon after the firefight at Niagara Falls State Park. From the look of it, Bolan surmised that most Buffalo residents were probably oblivious to the airport's existence. To make things safer yet, he'd bypassed the commercial line and booked a private charter flight from Jamestown to Detroit Metropolitan Airport. There, Zoe would have her choice of half a dozen airlines serving Southern California.

Their pilot—Rose MacDonald, owner-operator of Apex Airlines—was a thirtysomething redhead with an Aussie accent and a winning smile—at least, until she got a look at

Zoe's face. She started glaring daggers then, prepared to give the two male strangers holy hell, but Zoe saved them from a shouting match—or worse—by telling Rose that they were friends who'd rescued her from an obsessive stalker. She was going home to spend some time with family, Zoe explained, until the dust settled.

"I hope you fellas gave the scumbag some of his own medicine," the flygirl said, still angry, sounding dubious.

"I think he got the message," Johnny said. "But we may have to visit him again."

"If you do, give him a swift kick in the Jatz crackers for me, eh?"

"Be a pleasure," Johnny told her.

Bolan wasn't much on long goodbyes, and since he didn't know the lady, anyway, he left the send-off to his brother. Zoe had already thanked the Executioner half a dozen times, without asking his name, and he was glad to let it go at that.

The risk of any mafiosi trailing Zoe back to San Diego was, in Bolan's estimation, negligible. Vinnie Gallo had the resources to find out where she lived, of course, but he was in the middle of a crisis which, if Bolan had his way, was slated to become a full-scale meltdown. Putting out a contract through some other Family would be the last thing on his mind, assuming that the L.A. branch of *Cosa Nostra* was inclined to take the job or had hunters to spare.

No, Bolan had decided. Vinnie Gallo was about to be consumed by trouble in his own backyard.

They waited to see the Beechcraft Excalibur Queen Air lift off, circle once overhead, then strike a beeline westward, gaining altitude over Chautauqua Lake. When it was nearly out of sight and they were moving toward the car, Johnny declared, "She'll be all right."

"Should be," Bolan agreed.

"Tough losing family, though."

They'd learned that one firsthand, and it required no comment from the Executioner. Instead, he told his brother, "Gallo won't be happy with the way the trade went down."

"You got that right," Johnny replied. "He's out one under-boss and…how many guns?"

"Twenty-two on this round, by my count."

"He's running short of made men."

"Still a few left," Bolan said. "Plus mercenaries."

"And the cops."

That was a problem, Bolan recognized. And with the ranks of mafiosi thinning out in Buffalo, he'd have to find a way to deal with it.

Justice Building, Washington, D.C.

THE BIG FED grabbed the phone, his private line, before it finished ringing once. "Brognola."

"Hansen," said the Bureau's CID assistant director. "Got a minute?"

"Fire away."

"I sniffed around some more, that thing we talked about. Wasn't appreciated by the local field office, but they do what they're told most of the time. Since Boston, anyway."

He was referring to an old case, broken only at the turn of the new century, wherein some Boston G-man helped one of their Mafia informers frame four minor rivals for a murder he'd committed. Two of them had died in prison, while the other two emerged old, crippled men—and won a fat six-figure settlement that still would never make up for the time they'd lost. While that deal was unfolding, DOJ investigators learned that one of the agents involved had also fingered prosecution witnesses for hit teams, banking payoffs when the targets were eliminated. That agent served three years of a ten-year federal sentence, and was now locked up for forty, back in Massachusetts.

"So, you got something else?" Brognola asked.

"A guy on Buffalo PD who's been cooperative with the Bureau, to a point. He hates bad apples, but he won't go public. Sure as hell won't testify."

"Not my concern."

"Okay. Detective Sergeant Rudolph Arnold Mahan. Goes by 'Rudy,' so you don't get off on the wrong foot."

"He'll talk to me?" the big Fed asked.

"Can't speak for him," Hansen replied. "I wouldn't want to promise anything I can't deliver. Buffalo thinks Mahan may be having second thoughts about continuing collaboration. On the other hand, since Greg O'Malley screwed the pooch, he can't exactly put his head back in the sand, can he?"

"You never know. Thanks for the tip, regardless."

"Sure. I would say, 'Anytime,' but let's not make this thing a habit."

"Wouldn't dream of it," Brognola lied, and cut the link.

In his experience, the FBI had never learned the Golden Rule. Headquarters loved receiving information—solid leads or flimsy gossip, anything at all—but hated giving back. He knew that he'd incurred a debt with Hansen that would have to be repaid, and wondered how far he'd be tested when the time came.

A Buffalo detective, this one honest, if the Bureau's information could be trusted, wasn't prepared to break the wall of silence in a public way, but would help federal investigators weave a basket to contain some of the rotten apples on his team. Or was he? How could Brognola be sure this character wasn't corrupt, himself? It wouldn't be the first time that a dirty cop fed his competitors into the grinder, standing by to claim a bigger slice himself—or to protect someone above him.

On the plus side, he could talk to Mahan, feel him out, without exposing Bolan or his brother. Maybe play it off like he'd been a money trail for one of Vinnie Gallo's operations and noted the O'Malley hit, then checked with Buffalo regarding any semi-friendlies on the local force. He couldn't play it like he took for granted that the two of them were comrades. Mahan, by the time he'd made detective sergeant, would have seen the FBI in action, and he'd probably have some issues with the way they commandeered a case, throwing their weight around.

So, unobtrusive. Asking, without telling. Maybe hint something about an inside angle on the recent mayhem sweeping Buffalo?

No, leave that out. Whatever happened in the next few hours, he couldn't leave a trail of bread crumbs leading back to Justice, much less Stony Man.

Unless a miracle occurred, the Executioner was on his own.

Lower West Side, Buffalo

FRESH BACK FROM Jamestown, the Bolan brothers checked into a motel on South Park Avenue. The clerk who handled registration ignored their faces, didn't ask to see IDs and looked at "Matt Cooper's" Visa only long enough to make sure that the charge had cleared, before he passed it back. If he was on the lookout for a pair of guys ducking the Mob, he hid it well enough to rate an acting award.

"Room 18, far end, ground floor," he said, and pushed two keys across the grungy counter.

In the seedy room, the brothers spent an hour cleaning weapons and reloading magazines, talking through plans and watching live news broadcasts on the ancient Sony television set. The city and surrounding Erie County were in uproar over what the talking heads were calling the Niagara Massacre. Some of the dead had been identified, including Joseph Borgio, born Giuseppe, known to colleagues and a few reporters as "The Hammer." Lacking evidence of what had actually happened, they were reaching back through history to Russell Buffalino's era and the ancient raid at Apalachin, running old stock footage of the mafiosi from another time, long gone.

"They'll have Capone up next," Johnny said, topping off another 15-round magazine for his Glock.

"Wouldn't surprise me," Bolan said. "They have to justify their salaries."

"Good luck with that. You plan on calling Gallo back?"

"I want to let him stew awhile. Maybe rattle his cage a little more."

"Suits me. I'd still like to find out where Zoe's brother is."

"You may not find him, Johnny."

"Sure, I know. But—"

Bolan's cell phone rang. He checked the number before answering. "It's Hal," he said. Then, to the man from Washington, "What's up?"

"With the feed I'm getting from CNN, I should be asking you."

"Working some issues out," Bolan replied.

"Is there a resolution in our future?"

"Getting closer. Are you taking heat?"

"Not me. In fact," Brognola said, "I may have stumbled on to someone who can help you." He made it sound casual, when Bolan knew he had to have pulled every available string in an effort to help.

"I'm all ears," Bolan told his oldest living friend.

"They've got a sergeant of detectives there in Buffalo named Rudy Mahan. Word around the house is that he's fed up with a handful of the slugs, like that O'Malley. Not enough to testify, but if somebody caught him in the right mood..."

"Have you talked to him?"

"Not yet," Brognola said.

"Let me do that."

There was a silent pause, then, "Sure. If you think that's the way to go."

"No reason he should link you up to anything that's happened here," Bolan replied.

"Just so you know, I wouldn't mind."

"It's understood," Bolan said. "Thanks."

"Jesus. If we start to thank each other now, where does it end?" the big Fed asked.

"You're right. Scratch that."

"Okay. Is Johnny doing all right?"

"A-one. We're hoping to be out of here before much longer."

"That sounds like a plan. If you need anything..."

"I know. See you."

And that was all. Bolan turned back to Johnny, telling

him, "Turns out there may be someone on the force that we can talk to."

"Risky," Johnny said.

"I won't walk into anything that seems off-key."

"You mean, *we* won't."

"Same thing," Bolan said, as he grabbed a telephone directory out of the nearby nightstand, found a number and began to dial.

East Side, Buffalo

"THIS THING HAS gone to hell," Strauss said.

"Ya think?" Kelly replied.

"What kinda goat screw was that? They lose the girl, Joe Borgio, all those other guys—for what?"

"You said it. Goat screw."

"It makes me think we backed a losing horse, you know?"

Facing each other in a corner booth of a small mom-and-pop diner on Sycamore Street, with coffee on the table, Kelly eyed his partner, trying to figure out where Strauss was going with his gripe. No question, they were in the shit, but if Strauss thought he'd found a way out of the situation, he had kept it to himself so far.

"What are you getting at?" Kelly asked.

"Hey, I'm just thinking out loud. If the old man can't hold it together anymore, what the hell do we owe him?"

"It's not what we owe him," Kelly said. "It's what he's got on us that counts."

"And what's he gonna do with that?" Strauss asked, his voice lowered almost to a whisper. "Think the Feds are gonna deal with *him,* to take us down? If anything, it's gonna be the other way around."

"You wanna be a rat, now?"

"Who said that? My point is that if Mr. G. goes down, we aren't obliged to try to save him. What's he gonna say to put us on the spot? Confess that *he* told us to do some hits? That's life without parole, murder in aid of racketeering, right? They'd likely throw his ass in supermax."

"And how's life looking to you, after that?" Kelly asked. "Think we'd walk away from it? Pick up our pensions and retire to the Bahamas?"

"All I'm saying is—"

"We need to clean this up," Kelly said, interrupting him. "The *best* case, if he falls, we both go back to living on our salaries, no frills, with I.A. looking up our asses. No way the media will buy O'Malley as the only cop on the pad."

"All right. When you say clean it up, what did you have in mind?" Strauss asked.

"The girl, for one thing. She can nail us both for kidnapping."

"You're crazy if you think she's still in Buffalo."

"So, what? Airlines don't fly to San Diego anymore?"

"You're kiddin' me," Strauss said. "Head west and cap the broad, when all this other crap is going on? Just tell the captain, 'Hey, we thought we'd take a few vacation days'?"

"You want her out there, talking to the Feds?" Kelly asked.

There was no response to that, at first, then Strauss replied, "Well, *both* of us can't go."

"I'll do it."

"Just hang on a second. If she isn't running to the Feds already, don't you think she'll worry about someone finding her at home? She knows we got her phone number, for chrissakes. Can you see her sitting there eating popcorn, waiting for the knock?"

"Goddamn it!"

"Right. We need to get a tip on where she's gone, *then* roll her up."

"A tip from who?"

"Gallo's got someone in the D.A.'s office. We could start there."

"Hmm."

"If you've got something better…"

"No," Kelly admitted grudgingly. "You know his name?"

"I'll get it. Then, we have a little tit-a-tit."

"Rosetta Stone isn't working for you, partner."

"Women love it when I talk dat jive," Strauss said.

"Just get the number," Kelly told him, "or you'll be talking in the joint."

Buffalo Police Headquarters

RUDY MAHAN THOUGHT he'd picked the wrong time to quit smoking. Wrong week, month, year—any way you sliced it. He'd be better off if he bought stock in Nicorette and spent his dividends on Marlboros. Unless you listened to his doctor. In which case...

"Damn it!" Reaching for the phone before it shrilled at him a second time, Mahan prepared himself for more bad news.

What other kind was there?

"Mahan," he growled.

"That's *Sergeant* Mahan?" asked a voice he didn't recognize.

"The very same. Who's asking?"

"Would you like to get a handle on what's happening with Vinnie Gallo's Family?"

"I didn't catch your name."

Ignoring him, the caller pressed ahead. "It started with a missing person. Joseph Dirks. He was a contractor in Buffalo."

That name again. And then, the sister.

"You said *was* a contractor."

"He's dead now. We should really talk about this face-to-face."

"Okay. Why don't you come on by and—"

"I was thinking of a private meeting. Someplace where his killers won't be eavesdropping."

"If you're inferring—"

"That would be *implying,*" he caller said. "*You* infer. I'm saying it flat-out. You want more details on this line?"

"Can't say I like where this is going," Mahan answered.

"It's already gone," the stranger said. "One hit, for sure. At least two more attempted. Something's rotten in your house, Sergeant, but I was told it hadn't tainted you."

"I don't know who you're talking to, but—"

"Same folks you are, I imagine. More or less."

Mahan wasted a scowl on the phone in his hand. "Hey, I like a wild-goose chase as much as the next guy, but I've hit my quota of crazy for this week, okay? If you want to come by here and see me—"

"Could you call in Strauss and Kelly?" the stranger asked. "Makes it easier than going after them with warrants."

"Listen, now—"

"Joe Dirks," the caller said again. "Ask them what happened to him. Ask about his sister, while you're at it. She's alive, no thanks to Strauss and Kelly. Ask them what happened in the park, and why."

Mahan felt sick, but there was only one way he could play it on an open line. "If you have a complaint to file—"

"I've filed it," the caller said. "It's in your hands now. Take action, or stand back and keep out of the way."

"You can't just—"

Click.

"Goddamn it!"

Mahan punched *69 for last-call return, sat strangling the handset while it rang and rang and—

"What?"

"Who's this?" Mahan demanded.

"Who ya lookin' for?"

"I need your name!"

"Name's Yarta."

"*Yarta?* Yarta *what?*"

"Yarta go screw yo'self."

Click!

Red-faced and steaming, Mahan called downstairs to have his last incoming call traced to its source. Five endless minutes later, he heard back: a public pay phone near the riverfront.

Useless.

Kelly and Strauss. Good friends of Greg O'Malley, who was looking dirtier with every passing hour since his death.

There's no such thing as one bad apple, Mahan thought. Hell, every cop knew that. Unless you had some two-man force out in the sticks somewhere. In which case, if one cop was dirty, he figured they both were. One of very few things old Jack Webb got right, when he was preaching to the choir on *Dragnet*: police departments would always have problems, since they had to recruit from the human race.

"I don't need this," Mahan muttered to himself.

But at the moment, who else could he trust?

11

Calaguiro Estates, Niagara Falls, Ontario

"We all set, then?" Al Cavallaro asked.

"Ready to roll," Elio Mangano replied.

"You got it straight now, for the border?"

"Sure. No more than three guys to a car, and space them out so it don't look like a parade or something."

"And the guns?"

"Be waiting for them on the other side," Mangano said. "Don't worry about Customs."

Taking unreported weapons either way, across the border, was a serious offense. Already pissed about the call for troops to mop up Vinnie Gallo's mess, the last thing Cavallaro needed was to have the bulk of his garrison jailed overnight on some stupid gun-running charge.

"All right, then. Get them rolling," he said, "before Vin calls back, PMSing."

Mangano snorted at that. "Good one, Al."

"Don't repeat it!"

"Who, me? What if he asks when you'll be coming over?"

"I'll be there before he gets a chance to ask. Gino's driving me."

"The two of you, alone?"

"Why not?"

"I thought, with all that's going down…"

"It's back across the river," Cavallaro said. "Why the hell you think he needs our boys?"

"Not, sure."

"Go on, now. Hit the road."

It sucked big-time, Cavallaro thought, the whole damned thing. Of course, he *was* an underling of Vinnie Gallo's in the structure of the Family. Shit rolled downhill, and captains took their orders from the general. No big surprise there, but it rankled Cavallaro that his apple cart should be upset by trouble Gallo brought upon himself somehow, in Buffalo. They might be next-door neighbors, but it felt as if they lived in two distinct and separate worlds. Not just the easygoing atmosphere of Canada, although that helped to keep Al's blood-pressure below volcanic levels. Life was easier, seemed to run smoother, since he'd been dispatched across the river to Ontario.

And now, goddamn it, he was going back.

Into a war zone, yet.

Cavallaro tried to remember the last time he'd seen this kind of trouble in the Family, but came up empty. It was more like something from the bad old days, turf wars and stuff his old man used to talk about—but more so. Almost like—

"You ready, boss?" Gino Pinelli asked him, standing in the open office doorway.

"Yeah, let's do it," Cavallaro answered, rising from his desk.

"No heat, right?"

"Nothing."

Pinelli nodded, looking gloomy. "Hope they got some decent stuff across the river."

"Same stuff we got here," Cavallaro said. "Only more so."

"Weird freaking deal," Pinelli said. "This trouble coming out of nowhere."

"Trouble always comes from *somewhere,* Gino. We're just getting hit with someone else's mess, this time."

Pinelli made no reply to that. He was a soldier, knew his place and wouldn't comment on the foibles of a boss unless invited to, by his direct superior. Cavallaro thought he might have said too much already, but he'd only make things worse by warning Gino not to carry tales. A soldier ought to know that on his own, regardless.

Looked at in a different light, he thought that *trouble* was another word for *opportunity*. If Cavallaro caught a break or two, he could remind the boss that he was valuable to the Family, advance himself while he was saving Vinnie Gallo's bacon. And if Gallo had some bad luck of his own—if he should catch a bullet, say, before the dust settled—that could be a blessing in disguise. Clear out the top spot for a man who'd proved himself in crisis, when a cool head and a steady hand were what mattered the most.

Why not? Call it a battlefield promotion.

Cavallaro thought it couldn't hurt to keep his fingers crossed.

Niagara Square, Buffalo, New York

THE SQUARE MEAL was a place where Mahan could relax for half an hour, generally without seeing any other cops or having to talk shop while he was trying to digest a hasty lunch or dinner. He was known there—well enough to rate a smile, at least—but no one from the staff loomed over him, obsessively inquiring if his food was hot enough, tasted all right, et cetera. He always tipped a little more than usual, just for the privilege of being left alone.

Of course, he always sat facing the door, a cop thing, so he saw the tall man enter, glance around, then head directly for his table. He could be FBI, the way he dressed and carried himself, Mahan thought. He braced himself for the intrusion, putting on a sour face to greet the stranger.

"Sergeant Mahan?"

"Who are you?"

The stranger sat across from him, not waiting for an invitation. When the waitress passed their way, the tall man shook his head and she kept going.

"Sergeant—"

"Do I know you?"

"Only from our conversation on the phone," his uninvited guest replied.

Mahan wondered if he could reach the Glock 19 on his right hip, and noted at the same time that the stranger wore some kind of pistol in a shoulder rig, beneath his right armpit. The jacket was unbuttoned, as was Mahan's, but he didn't feel like setting off a quick-draw contest in the middle of a busy restaurant.

"So, that was you," he said.

"I figured we could speak more freely where the walls don't have so many ears."

"And I can't call for backup."

"You're at no risk, Sergeant. That's a promise."

"Right. And I should trust you, since we go way back and all."

"I don't shoot cops. It's just a rule I have." He tossed it out, like someone else might say they disliked broccoli or mayonnaise.

"Okay," Mahan replied. "Who *do* you shoot?"

"Depends. Today, it's soldiers from the Gallo Family."

"And you're confessing to me...why?"

"Wrong word. 'Confessing' indicates a sense of guilt. I'm *warning* you that what's been happening around your city isn't finished yet. *Advising* you that certain people on your squad are playing for the other team."

"And you know this because...?"

"It's obvious. But if I need to spell it out, let's start with Gregory O'Malley. He was killed trying to carry out a hit for Vinnie Gallo. I imagine you've already worked that out, even if you're afraid to say it publicly."

"I'm not afraid of—"

"Michael Strauss and Leonard Kelly kidnapped Zoe Dirks from her hotel." The stranger plowed ahead, cutting him off. "They would have murdered her and planted her somewhere, but I persuaded Gallo to exchange her for his underboss."

"Joe Borgio in the park. You did all that?"

"Somebody on their side forgot the terms of our agreement. There's a price for that."

"And more to come," Mahan said.

"Absolutely. What *you* need to do is clean your own house, or the Feds will do it for you. You already know they're building cases, but rats like Strauss and Kelly could destroy the PD from within, if they decided to go down fighting. Maybe telling tales."

"They're not alone," Mahan replied.

"In a department this size? Not a chance. Smart money says you have the others pegged."

"I'm not a rat."

"No. You're a law-enforcement officer. Time to decide if that means anything."

The stranger rose. Mahan leaned toward him, saying, "Hey! I can't just let you go now, after all this murder talk."

"Do what you have to do," the tall guy said, turning his back.

Mahan sat watching, meat loaf soured in his stomach, as the stranger left the restaurant and disappeared.

KELLY HAD NEVER met the assistant D.A. his partner claimed was taking payoffs from the Gallo Family. He was surprised to hear the name—Seth Kantor—and discover that the guy wasn't an Eyetie, but so what? Money corrupted everybody, right? Kelly was living proof of that.

He'd called ahead, made an appointment with the assistant D.A., and went alone, leaving Strauss out of it. His partner was a big help when it came to muscle work, but making nice with strangers definitely wasn't his strong suit. The last thing Kelly wanted, seeking information from the prosecutor's office, was to piss somebody off.

Seth Kantor's office was a fourth-floor cubbyhole with no receptionist. He'd have to share somebody from the steno pool with other assistant district attorneys, maybe file writs and motions on his own. The harried look on Kantor's face told Kelly that he wasn't happy to be meeting with a cop who knew his dirty little secret.

Tough. They all had things to hide, right? That was life.

"Detective Kelly?"

"Mr. Kantor. Thanks for making time."

"It sounded urgent."

"Absolutely."

"So?" Meaning, *Get on with it and stop wasting my time.*

"We've had a witness in a missing person case drop out of sight," Kelly explained. "Before she took a powder she was acting crazy, going on about conspiracies, accusing the police of being in on some big plot against her family. I need a heads-up if she contacts anybody from your office, so that we can get her proper care. Before she hurts herself, you know… or someone else."

"And this affects our mutual acquaintance?"

"He'd be one of those she'd finger, definitely," Kelly said.

"And you, I take it."

Shrugging that one off, he said, "No telling where it might wind up."

Kantor grabbed a pen. "Name?"

"Zoe Dirks."

"You want to spell that for me?"

Kelly did, adding, "She's out of Dago."

"Pardon me?"

"That's San Diego. California?"

"I'm familiar with it. And she's gone back there?"

"Beats me. She didn't leave a forwarding address."

"Are you expecting her to call some other agency?"

"I couldn't rule it out."

The prosecutor grimaced. "If it comes to that, you realize I can't be any help to you."

"I figured that. But if you get a lead…"

"You'll be the first to know."

"Appreciate it."

Kelly rose to leave. The assistant D.A. delayed him, saying, "And it goes both ways, right? If you hear something pertaining to this office, or…"

"I've got your number," Kelly said, and left the cubicle.

Strike two, he thought. If Zoe Dirks called anybody, it would likely be the FBI. The first he heard about it would be when they showed up with a warrant to arrest him. Maybe it was time to put his papers in, put out some lie about the stress wearing him down, and get the hell away from Buffalo while there was time.

If there was time.

But that meant leaving Vinnie Gallo in the lurch, which was more dangerous than dealing with the Feds. If nothing else, Kelly knew he should tidy up his mess before he hit the road. And if he couldn't manage that, he'd have to find someplace to hide where even Gallo couldn't find him.

Greenland, maybe. Or Antarctica.

South Buffalo, New York

"THE IRISH MOB? Getting distracted, are we?" Johnny asked.

"Not even," Bolan answered. "Gallo gets along with them, but only just. They kick back tribute and the wheels go 'round—until today."

"We're monkey-wrenching?"

"That's the ticket. Leave them pissed off at the Family. It's one more headache for the godfather."

"Okay," Johnny replied. "So we'll need witnesses."

"At least one, fit to carry tales."

The Shamrock Social Club stood on Abbott Street, northwest of Cazenovia Park. It was the main hangout for members of an outfit run by Kevin Shaughnessy and Brian Devlin, minor but ferocious lords of crime within the confines of their turf. The Mob wasn't a large one, but it didn't need to be. Each member was a stone-cold killer in his own right, and a simple warning normally persuaded any opposition to depart for safer climes.

Officially, the Shamrock Social Club accepted any members who could demonstrate a solid Irish ancestry, but no one from the straight world ever bothered to apply. They'd pass

by, smiling, nodding to the hoods out front, but no outsider
crossed the threshold without a specific invitation from one
of the men in charge.

Again—until today.

Bolan parked a quarter block west of the club and walked
back, Johnny at his side. They both had silenced weapons underneath their light raincoats, their right hands clutching pistol
grips through pockets opened with a knife blade. At twenty
yards and closing, Bolan saw the three punks standing guard
push off from where they had been leaning on the wall, turning to block the entrance with their bodies.

"Coppers, is it?" one of them inquired, going for a hidden weapon.

"Not even close," Bolan replied, and shot him in the face.

Johnny caught the second reaching for a gun he'd never
have a chance to use, then both of them shot number three as
he was bolting for the Shamrock's entrance, to alert the customers inside. He struck the door face-first, with force enough
to hurt if he'd still been alive, and bounced back for an awk-
ward landing on the pavement.

Bolan stepped across the bodies, pushed in through the
door with Johnny at his heels. A dozen faces turned in their
direction, male without exception, their expressions caught
somewhere between surprise and anger. Staring down the
muzzles of a Steyr AUG and Bolan's Spectre, no one risked
a move.

"Where's Brian Devlin?" Bolan asked the room at large.
"And Kevin Shaughnessy?"

A balding heavyweight to Bolan's left sneered, "Never
heard of them."

"Too bad," Bolan said, and his M4 spit three rounds that
turned the fat man into lifeless suet on the slide.

"Let's try again!"

"Feck off wi' yeh," another Shamrock patron snarled, rising and reaching for what had to be a sidearm under his jacket.

Johnny handled that one with a tidy double-tap, the second
round impacting as his target toppled over backward, spilling

pints of Guinness beer from the table he shared with two more goons. That pair sat frozen, murder in their eyes.

"Nobody wants to talk? Then listen," Bolan told his captive audience. "You mess with Vinnie Gallo, there's a tab to pay. Collection starts right here, right now."

The nine or ten survivors lunged for cover as he raked the room, firing a foot or so above their ducking heads, with Johnny's assault rifle joining in. Nobody tried returning fire. They were too busy scrambling for their lives.

A minute later, jogging toward the Mercury, Johnny said, "That should stir things up."

"Open another front, at least," Bolan replied. "Now we just need a little color in the mix."

Buffalo Police Headquarters

"The Irish now? What sense does that make?" Rudy Mahan asked.

"What sense does *any* of it make?" Eugene Franks replied.

Mahan could have explained it to him—most of it, at least—but that would open up too many doors. He wasn't sure what lay behind some of them yet, and wanted no more rude surprises added to the crap already on his plate.

"No comment from the Shamrock, I suppose?"

"They'd rather eat ground glass," Franks said.

"That's wishful thinking."

"Was it Gallo's people, you suppose?"

"Could be."

And that was true. It *could* be Vinnie Gallo lashing out at Shaughnessy and Devlin, maybe blaming them for all his recent troubles, but if Mahan had to bet, he would've put his money on the guy who'd spoiled his lunch and left him with a killer case of heartburn. Mr. No-name with the graveyard eyes, roping the Irish in on his vendetta... Why?

"You ever see this kind of shit go down before, Sarge?"

"Nope. This is a new one, and I hope I never see the likes of it again."

The worst part, what he couldn't say to Franks, was having dirty cops right in the middle of it ready to drag the whole department down. That kind of scandal never went away. Losing the people's trust like that could do irreparable harm.

"I want the boy-os in here," Mahan ordered. "Devlin, Shaughnessy, ASAP. They won't say squat, but if we keep them tied up for a while, maybe they won't contribute to the body count."

"More wishful thinking, Sarge?"

"Why not? It's all we've got to go with."

"Right. I'll roust them, if they haven't gone to ground already."

Just what I need, thought Mahan. Add a real gang war on top of Mr. X and his vendetta tearing up the town.

Mahan wished he had a number for the stranger, worried at the same time by the big guy's knowledge of his conversations with the FBI. There was a leak somewhere, and if the word got back to headquarters, Mahan would find himself on everybody's shit list, whether they were clean or dirty. If he got a rat jacket, he might as well pack in the job and go out shopping for a new career. A Walmart greeter, maybe, with the flair he had for making people feel at ease.

As if.

"Hey, Sarge!" Leland Wilkey called as he double-timed down the hallway toward where Mahan stood. "You hear what's poppin' on the East Side?"

"Spill it, Lee."

"Somebody just kicked the hell out of the Clinton Street Commandos. Four, five dead, and counting."

"Crips? Bloods? Who?" Mahan demanded.

"None of the above. Word is, it was a couple white guys, claimed to work for Vinnie Gallo."

"Jesus jumping Christ!"

The young detective blinked at him. "You all right, Sarge?"

"Ask me tomorrow," Mahan said. "If both of us are still around."

Clinton Street, East Side, Buffalo

"I GUESS YOU meant it," Johnny said.

"What's that?"

"Adding some color to the mix."

The district wasn't quite a ghetto, but its complexion had changed over time, from predominantly Polish to largely African-American. Ornate nineteenth-century churches shared the streets with modest wood-frame cottages, many a story and a half, with smaller rear additions that produced a telescope effect. Say 95 percent of East Side's residents were law-abiding citizens; that still left 5 percent engaged in crime that ranged from petty theft to drug-dealing, extortion, hijacking and murder. Six or seven gangs claimed turf around the East Side. Bolan needed only one.

The toughest he could find.

"Looks like the place," Johnny observed.

A smallish corner house had been fortified. The front door, underneath its layer of paint, was steel. Ditto the window shutters. Inside, he guessed there would be sandbags, maybe mattresses around the walls, for insulation against drive-by shooters. Patchwork on the outer stucco walls commemorated strafings from the past. No lookouts were apparent, but that didn't mean they weren't on duty.

"No way we can fake it in this neighborhood," Johnny said.

"Straight up the middle, then," Bolan replied. "You set?"

He got a nod in answer, made a U-turn in the middle of the block and stopped outside the Clinton Street Commandos' clubhouse. Both of them were on the pavement in a heartbeat, Johnny with his Steyr, Bolan with the Milkor MGL in hand, his Spectre M4 slung. He had a 40 mm HE round up first, and sent it hurtling toward the steel door while they stood at curbside, hunched and waiting for the blast.

It took only the one round, but he followed up with two more, blowing in the two front windows, choking the bungalow with smoke and plaster dust. It was a short run from the sidewalk to the yawning doorway, with people in the house dazed and cursing, some down, some stagger-lurching for the nearest weapons. Bolan switched guns as he entered, stuttering short bursts of Parabellum rounds, aiming to wound more often than he killed.

"You mess with Vinnie Gallo, this is what you get!" he

shouted, firing as he moved from room to room. "Remember it!"

Some would. The living, anyway.

A few rounds of return fire crackled through the battle fog, suppressed when Bolan or his brother sighted on the muzzle-flashes. Anybody who could run was headed out the back way, scattering. Bolan ignored them, let them go, bearing the word. Within the hour, everyone in East Side would be talking up the raid, most of them horrified, a few plotting revenge against the Gallo Family.

"We done?" Johnny asked.

"Almost."

Bolan raised the Milkor, aimed it toward the ceiling and released a pyrotechnic round into the half-attic above. Flames blossomed instantly, smoke pouring from the ragged vent he'd opened. He retreated, then, toward the exit, yelling at the fallen as he passed.

"Get up!" he bellowed. "Hit the bricks, before you're toasted! It's a fire sale, courtesy of Vinnie Gallo! Don't forget it!"

Those who made it out would not.

When they were rolling, smoke and flames receding in the rearview, angry faces swiveling to track the Mercury, Johnny eased back into his seat and asked, "You think they'll bite?"

"White shooters, dropping Gallo's name? At the very least they'll want to check it out."

"It's race war, then."

"A thug war," Bolan answered. "If it gets that far."

His brother looked across at him, half smiling, said, "You've got something in mind."

"I might at that," the Executioner replied.

12

North Forest Acres, Buffalo

"*My* name? The rotten pricks are using *my* name?"

"All over town, Vin," Jerry Portoghesi said. "Hitting the Irish and the bla—"

"I know who they've been hitting," Vinnie Gallo snapped. "But blaming *me?* What the hell is that—"

He saw it, then, as plain as day, and it made perfect sense. He hadn't cracked, despite all that the rotten sons of bitches had thrown at him, both sides of the border, so they'd changed their strategy. Now they were hitting other gangs in Buffalo and blaming Gallo's Family, making it look as if he'd lost it and was lashing out at anybody he could reach. Hoping the Irish and whoever else they stirred up would strike back at Gallo—which, he thought, the idiots were likely stupid and pissed off enough to try.

"Goddamn. It's smart, that's what it is."

"What's that, Vin?"

"These guys know their stuff. I give them that," Gallo said. "What we need to do is head this off before we wind up fighting every two-bit clique in town."

"Do you have a plan, Vin?"

"Jesus, you're my frigging *consigliere.* You're supposed to help me think of plans, eh? But in answer to your question, yeah, I got a plan."

"Okay, so—"

"You get on the phone," Gallo said. "Talk to Shaughnessy or Devlin. Both is better, if you can. And who's the top dog for that East Side outfit?"

"A guy named Cletus Washington," Portoghesi said. "His homeys call him Rocket."

"Homeys?"

"I'm just saying."

"Call him, too. Tell all of them we had nothing to do with any of their people getting hit. Explain the best you can, without divulging any Family secrets, eh?"

"Okay. What if they don't believe me?"

"Be persuasive, Jerry. What in hell do I pay you for?"

"Right, Vin."

"And if you can't persuade them, then I guess we've got to kill them."

"All of them?"

"Al will be here pretty quick, with extra soldiers. These micks and whatever, at least we've got a pretty fair idea of where to find them."

Nothing like the bastards who'd been kicking Gallo's ass, so far.

"I got weapons waiting for the backup team," Portoghesi said. "And some places they can stay."

"Screw that. I didn't call them over here to sit around and take a nap. I want them on the street, first thing, and Al, too. I don't want him thinking he's too big to get his hands dirty."

"He won't like that, coming from me."

"He doesn't have to *like* it," Gallo answered. "He just has to *do* it."

"Right, Vin. Sure."

"Now, get on those calls, before somebody else starts taking potshots at us, will you?"

"On my way, Vin."

Gallo hated feeling any kind of sneaking admiration for his enemies. Ideally, he preferred to think of them as insects he could flick aside or crush under his Bruno Magli loafers, then forget. Raw contempt had served him well for years, but there had been a time or two—

Forget that!

Gallo already had enough grief as it was, without exhuming ugly memories from decades past. He hadn't gotten where he was without eliminating certain worthy adversaries. Names and reasons didn't matter now. What counted was his present trouble, which—thanks to the quick wits of his latest enemies—was only getting worse.

But he could change that, sure. He was a born survivor, and the day he went down—keeping it in mind that *everyone* went down sometime, somehow—he'd go down fighting. Stupid pricks would have to pry his jaws open, to get them off some dying bastard's throat.

Go out in style. Damn right.

South Buffalo

"PHONE FOR YOU, Kev," Rory Keegan said.

"Who the hell is it?" Kevin Shaughnessy demanded.

"One of Gallo's greasers, if you can believe it."

"Is it, now?" Shaughnessy took his time deciding whether he should laugh or cuss a blue streak, then said, "All right. Give it here."

The cordless phone changed hands. "You got a feckin' lot of nerve, calling this number."

"How else am I supposed to talk to you?" the caller asked.

"Try begging for your worthless life when I'm there, standing over yer fat carcass with a cleaver."

"Listen, Kevin—"

"Friends, are we? Bosom feckin' buddies?"

"Huh?"

"Feel free to call me Mr. Shaughnessy."

"Oh, right. So, this is all a big mistake."

"You dagos made it!"

"Hey, now. There's no call for—"

"Shooting up the Shamrock, killing half a dozen of my

boys. Don't try to make it sound like you forgot the sugar with my tea."

"It wasn't us!" his caller blurted out.

"It wasn't, eh? A couple Eyetie looking feckers just decided that they'd take your goombah's name in vain?"

"That's it, exactly."

"Bullshit. Just because yer stupid doesn't mean *I* am."

"Listen, will you? If you've been awake the past two days, you know that we've been getting hit ourselves."

"And one of you without a lick of sense decided it was me and Brian done it, so you sent a couple of your wops—"

"I'm warning you."

"Oh, yeah? You kill my boys, and now yer *warning* me? Feck you!"

He cut the link and turned to Keegan, took a second to compose himself, then asked, "Where's Brian?"

"Talking to the families."

"All right. I need him back here, quick-like. Tell him there's no time to lose."

"Got it." Keegan was dialing as he turned away, already speaking as he cleared the room.

Shaughnessy still couldn't believe the arrogance. No, scratch that. He could easily *believe* it, coming from the Gallo crowd, but what he couldn't do was *swallow* it. If Gallo or his flunky thought they could roll onto Irish turf, raise hell, then lay the blame on someone else, their brain cells weren't connected.

Shaughnessy and Devlin didn't have the biggest gang in Buffalo, by any means, but they were known for their ferocity. They'd lost six of their men so far, but Gallo had been hit much harder, if the word on the street was accurate. There'd never be a better time to knock the cocky mafioso off his high horse, taking full advantage of the losses he had suffered, striking while the iron was hot.

Shaughnessy's Irish eyes weren't smiling at the moment, but they *would* be, when he'd personally pumped a few bullets into Vinnie Gallo's head and watched the blood run out his ears.

Some bosses lost their touch as they went up the ladder, leaving all the dirty work to others, but that wasn't—and had never been—the Irish way. Go back to Vincent Coll, Legs Diamond, Dean O'Banion in Chicago, down to Whitey Bulger in South Boston. All of them had kept their hands in, killing when they had to, setting an example for their soldiers.

All of them were *dead,* of course—except for Bulger, on his way to prison after fifteen years or something on the lam—but they had gone down swinging, taking other bastards with them, just like Jimmy Cagney in the movies.

And that, Shaughnessy thought, with a degree of pleasure that surprised him, was the only way to go.

East Side, Buffalo

ROCKET WAS RAGING. Pacing up and down his crib with long strides, not quite jitterbugging, but the angry-nervous walk that friends and family had long since come to know as warning signs of an explosion in the offing. He'd been that way forever—well, as far back as he could remember, anyway, around the time his pops left, *way* before the man at East High kicked him out for taking down that shop teacher. Pig had it coming, but they had to give the lecture: "Cletus Washington, you've gone too far this time!"

Sometimes he wondered how they'd like him now.

No time for skating down memory lane today, though.

A couple of ofays came onto his turf, blew his peeps away, and told the others it was from Vinnie frigging Gallo. What the hell was *that* about, and how did they expect to get away with it?

Rocket heard a phone blare out a Tupac ring tone, sounded like "Thug Passion," and he caught a sidelong glimpse of Little Puppet answering. And seconds later: "Rocket, man. For you."

"Who is it?"

"Dunno."

"Well, find out!"

Low-pitched mumbling, then, "He's one of Gallo's. The conspiglatory. Somethin'."

"Jesus. Gimme that!" He grabbed the phone. "Who the hell is dis?"

"I told your boy," the caller said. "I'm Mr. Gallo's *consigliere,* calling you at his instruction to explain the recent incident."

"Wasn't no goddamn *incident!* Couple your shooters come up in here, killin' friends of mine an' burnin' down the house!"

"I know what happened, but you need to understand we had no part in that."

"Man's bustin' caps and drops your boss's name? You got no part in dat? You shittin' me!"

"It's a confusing thing, I know, but—"

"Hell wi' dat! You be the only one *confused,* thinkin' I'd buy some line an' let ya off the hook."

"Look, we don't want—"

"Y'all think I give a rat's ass *what* you want? You struck a fire, and your boss is gonna be the one gets burned!"

He broke the link and tossed the phone to Little Puppet, snapping orders out while it was still in flight. "Call ever'body!" he commanded. "It be time for us to *mobilize.* Baby Commandos, too. I want 'em all strapped. Pull out ever'thing we got and put it on the street. We gonna show them muthas what it mean to mess wid someone else's thing."

His men were scrambling by the time he finished, rushing off to do as they'd been told. They'd all lost friends in the attack on Clinton Street, and payback was a bitch. Especially for those on the receiving end.

And it was going to be a superbitch, this time.

Someone was always getting killed around the East Side, for one reason or another, but they hadn't had an all-out war in something like two years. Rocket had been expecting something, wondering how it would start, but going up against the Gallos was a trip. It might have worried him at one time, but they'd started it. Now that the fat was in the fire, he didn't mind the thought of taking it uptown, dropping it right on Gallo's doorstep. Teach him how the brothers in the 'hood rolled, when you pissed them off.

Rocket was soaring, goddamn straight.

And when he landed, he might set the whole damn town on fire.

North Forest Acres, Buffalo

"YOU NAILED IT," Johnny said. "The plates are all Canadian. Ontario."

"It figured that he'd call for reinforcements," Bolan told him.

"I count nineteen, so far. May not be all of them."

"It's plenty," Bolan answered, peering downrange through the Barrett's AN/PVS-10 scope. "Ear plugs."

His own were already in place, a pair of SureFire Ear-Pro Sonics Defenders, barely visible at any distance. With so many marks to choose from, Bolan picked at random, settling the reticle on a face distinguished by its sneer below a pair of Gucci sunglasses. He squeezed the Barrett's trigger, rode the recoil, and the sneering face exploded.

Shift. Acquire another target. Squeeze.

A second skull evaporated, while the headless zombie from his first shot did a jerky little two-step, then collapsed into a heap, as if his bones had turned to sawdust. Others in the killing zone were scrambling for their lives, the Barrett's booming voice now audible, a second after the first hit.

Shift. Spot the runner. Fire.

Round three ripped through a barrel chest, the .50-caliber projectile bursting lungs and heart, exiting through a shoulder blade with force enough to nearly disarticulate the dead man's arm. He went down flopping, blood and mutilated tissue flying everywhere.

Still eight rounds in the magazine, since once again he'd started with the chamber loaded. For his next shot, Bolan sighted on the hood of a crew wagon with Ontario plates, estimating where a round would find the fuel pump. Impact from the .50 BMG round drilled the hood and left a fist-size dent before it struck a spark inside and sent a fireball wafting toward the power lines above.

Now soldiers were emerging from the nearby house, some bringing two guns with them, tossing one to new arrivals, who had come unarmed. With seven rounds to spend before reloading, Bolan ranged among them, striking here and there with no discernible pattern in mind.

He caught a runner in midstride and gave him wings— until the flying corpse slammed head-on into Gallo's wall of cinder blocks and stained them with his blood.

The Executioner gut-shot a mafioso who had caught an M4 carbine on the fly and stood exposed, scanning the block for targets, trying to return fire. He then hit one of the soldiers running from the house, and spun him like a weather vane, before his feet got tangled up, knees gave and he dropped twitching to the pavement.

Next Bolan nailed two for one when they lined up just right, by accident, his full-metal-jacket round shattering one skull, then ripping through another soldier's throat to leave him coughing crimson through an ugly blowhole. Another gunner was sent tumbling through a crazy backward somersault across the hood of another crew wagon, bouncing once before he rolled out of sight.

Three-quarters of a gunman's face was sheared off, spraying the tattered fragments over two or three shooters standing around him, so that one keeled over, vomiting.

A final shot from the Barrett caught a Gallo soldier in the boss's doorway, picked him up and blew him back inside the house to soil the carpet.

"Good enough for now," the Executioner said, and lifted off the scope. "We'll let them clean up while the neighbors tie up 911."

Back to the car, at an easy jog, and they were out of there with no one to oppose them. Residents of ritzy neighborhoods might be skeet shooters, kill a pheasant or a grouse from time to time or keep a shiny pocket pistol in the nightstand for emergencies. The ones who'd rush outdoors to face a stranger carrying a .50 caliber Barrett were few and very far between.

Like, none at all.

"I'm guessing the *padrino*'s pissed," Johnny said.

Bolan smiled, then replied, "He ain't seen nothing yet."

"THIS HAS ABSOLUTELY gotten out of hand."

"I hear ya, Sarge," Eugene Franks replied.

It wasn't quite the worst Mahan had seen, since coming on the job. There'd been car wrecks, of course, and people set on fire. A crazy woman who had cut a baby from its mother's stomach after half a dozen doctors said she couldn't have her own. But shootingwise, he thought the bloody scene outside Vincent Gallo's house came closest to the prize.

Against the numbers and the blood, of course, he had to weigh the fact that all the dead were first-rate scumbags, likely murderers themselves, who had deserved exactly what they got. Officially, however, the identity of any given murder victim carried no weight when it came to diligently turning over every rock, to find the perp responsible.

Except, in this case, Mahan thought he had a pretty fair idea who'd done the deed.

A guy with graveyard eyes who'd sat across a table from him at The Square Meal, not so long ago.

"How many?" Mahan asked.

"Nine dead," Franks answered, "plus a couple who got singed around the edges when the car went up."

"Then he, whoever, just stopped shooting?"

"Bagged his limit, maybe."

"I'd be very much surprised if that were true."

"Okay, then. Say the big gun's making too much noise. He spooked and split before the first squad showed."

"Lucky for them."

But in his head, Mahan could almost hear the stranger telling him, *"I don't shoot cops. It's just a rule I have."*

"You think the Irish did this?" Franks inquired. "Or maybe Clinton Street?"

"It's possible," Mahan said, knowing better. He'd be stunned to find that either outfit had a shooter of this quality, and both were likely still in shock from the attacks they'd suffered in the past two hours. Mahan thought they *would* be hitting back, but it would take a little longer, and they likely wouldn't be this organized. Drive-bys, maybe. Or a car bomb.

"You seen the boss yet?" Mahan asked.

"Not home," Franks told him. "And before you ask me, yes, we checked the case. Proximate cause, looking for victims, weapons, yada-yada."

"Where'd he go?"

"His mouthpiece claims nobody knows."

"Uh-huh. And if you buy that—"

"Brooklyn Bridge," Franks said, beating him to it.

"Job one," Mahan said, "is finding Vinnie Gallo. If we don't, somebody else is bound to. Shaughnessy or Devlin, Clinton Street, whoever did this. Till we clear it up, the Gallo Family is tops on the endangered species list."

"You say that like you figure it's a bad thing, Sarge."

"What I think doesn't matter, Gene. We get the big bucks to prevent crimes, not encourage them."

"Big bucks, my—"

"Anyway, get somebody checking deeds to property for anything with Gallo's name on it. The very least, we need to question him about this turkey shoot."

"You're thinking something like protective custody?"

"Can't force him into it, but if he asks…"

"That's rich. Bum spends his whole life ripping people off and killing anyone who's in his way, and now we're supposed to *save* his ass?"

"Serve and protect," Mahan reminded Franks.

"Yeah, yeah."

"Hey, Strauss and Kelly didn't get the squeal on this?"

"I couldn't say."

"There's something I need to ask them," Mahan told Franks. "If you see them sometime…"

"Sure. I'll make a note."

"Meanwhile, let's try to get these bodies out of here ASAP, so all the happy rich folks can enjoy their view."

13

Black Rock, Buffalo, New York

"Nice welcome you give us, Vinnie." Al Cavallaro, his forehead bandaged, glared angrily at Gallo.

"You think I set that up?" Gallo replied. "That's crazy talk."

"You let us walk into it. What's the difference?"

"You knew damn well what I've been going through and why I called you. Now you got a taste of it yourself. If all you can do is complain, maybe I need another capo for across the river."

Cavallaro winced at that, then said, "Tell me what I'm suppose to do with half my men."

"*My* men," Gallo reminded him. "And you're suppose to lead them by example. Let them know that metal sliver took your eyebrow off, and not your balls."

Gallo had missed the fireworks at his main house in North Forest Acres, having pulled back to the Black Rock hardsite for security. Surrounded by a six-foot wall, it covered fifteen wooded acres between Tonawanda Street and the Scajaquada Expressway. All but a handful of the Family's remaining troops were now inside the wall, making Gallo feel like an old feudal lord under siege.

And he didn't like it. Not a goddamned bit.

"Okay, if it's balls you want, it's balls you get," Cavallaro said. "What's the play?"

"Tonight," Gallo replied, "we button up and sit right here.

Tomorrow, we put every set of eyes we got out on the street. We sweep from Riverside to Kaisertown, through every neighborhood along the way. Tap every source and follow up on every lead. Reward the people who play ball with us, and punish them that don't."

"Take back the town, in other words."

"In those *exact* words," Gallo said.

"So, what about the Micks and Clinton Street?"

"That wasn't us."

"*They* seem to think it was."

"I got my *consigliere* working on it."

"Jerry. So, has he convinced them yet?"

"I said he's working on it!"

"Okay, if you say so." Cavallaro spread his open hands. "I'd like to know, when I get out there, am I gonna get my ass shot off by Irish, blacks or whoever in hell took down *your* men, outside *your* house in broad daylight."

"Somebody gives you any grief, you put them down," Gallo said. "Makes no difference if they're white, black, green, whatever. Kill a freaking leprechaun if you like."

"So, a bloodbath."

"It wasn't my idea. I didn't start it, but I plan to finish it."

"I'll brief the boys," Cavallaro said. "Get them fired up for tomorrow."

"Tell them when it's done, we'll have a party like the old days. Celebrate the victory."

"Will do."

"Alley, I hope you got my back on this."

"Vin, I been covering your back for twenty years."

"Just so you remember who's in charge."

"How likely am I to forget?"

Not likely, Gallo thought, with me reminding you. Part of a boss's job, the way he saw it, was keeping underlings in line. It wasn't easy, though, when somebody kept hammering the Family, and Gallo couldn't find out who in hell they were, much less get rid of them. It was a poor reflection on his leadership and had to be corrected soon, before the *Cosa Nostra* sharks smelled blood and started circling.

Like Cavallaro, it was time for Callo to remind his peers that he had balls. And brains.

And guns, of course. Still lots and lots of guns.

Justice Building, Washington, D.C.

"I'M WATCHING IT on CNN right now," Brognola told his caller, Aaron Kurtzman, phoning in from Stony Man.

"It's getting worse," Kurtzman said.

"Always does, before the fever breaks."

On-screen the printed crawl updated him on Buffalo's body count. Footage showed EMTs hoisting bagged corpses into a meat wagon, outside the home of "alleged mobster" Vincent Gallo. The segment's talking head, a seriously flirty blonde, reported that Gallo had not been at home when the fireworks went off.

"Feels like we ought to do…something," Kurtzman commented.

"It's unofficial," Brognola reminded him. "Unsanctioned. Personal."

"I get it, but—"

"But nothing. I've already got the Bureau with its nose stuck in. As much as it hurts, we need to let this run its course."

There was a brief silence on the line, and then, "Okay. It's your call."

"The only call," Brognola said. "It's not the first time we've been through something like this."

"You're right. Barbara said the same."

Mission controller Barbara Price, the Farm's heart and soul. She was Bolan's lover, at times, but she still made the hard calls.

"There you go," Brognola said. "Anything else?"

"We think the thing in Venezuela's nearly done. It looks all right."

"Good news, then. Keep me posted."

And, as usual, they broke it off without goodbyes. Within the savage world they occupied, a person never knew when one of those was going to be permanent.

The twelve-step programs pushed a plan of living one day at a time. In Brognola's world—make that Bolan's world, which the big Fed had entered full-time when their operation went legit—the focus was on getting through one hour at a time, often one minute at a time. Some made it; others didn't. Bolan had survived this far on guts, experience, audacity and heart. But he was only human, after all.

And someday, he'd run out of time.

Would it be Buffalo, with brother Johnny fighting at his side? Would some reporter ultimately trace the younger Bolan's background and write a weepy retrospective piece about how tragedy had come full-circle?

Not if Brognola had anything to say about it.

But he wasn't planning for a wake right now. In spite of what he'd said to Kurtzman, he was looking for a way to help and still cover his ass. More accurately, cover Stony Man—which, in Brognola's mind, like the proverbial show, must go on.

Maybe a call to Buffalo, to a specific sergeant of detectives. He could dance around the fine points, let the sarge know he was in the midst of something that he didn't want to mess with. But a good cop wouldn't swallow that. He'd want the details, and when those were not forthcoming, he'd go out to find them on his own. Maybe get killed while he was doing it—or worse, find out enough to guarantee he *would* be killed.

The day it came to that, Brognola thought, he'd pull the pin.

Maybe. Or would he manage to accommodate that, too?

We live and learn.

Sometimes, the lessons make us wonder if we've lived too long.

South Buffalo

"WE READY?" Brian Devlin asked.

"As ready as we'll ever be," Kevin Shaughnessy replied. "Thirty-one men, all mad as hell about their mates."

"And packed?"

"Two guns apiece, the minimum. We dug out ever'thing we've got, down to the Thompson out of Tom McGinty's rec room."

"Jesus, that old fossil."

"Tommy, or the Thompson?"

"Take your pick," Devlin said.

"It can shoot and he can handle it. They're in."

"God bless them, then, and welcome."

"So, you found the dagos?"

"Where we thought."

"Black Rock," Shaughnessy said, not making it a question.

"Walled up with their lord and master."

"Numbers whittled down before they even got there."

"They'll be blaming us for that, as well," Devlin said.

"Christ, I hope so. Let them get so scairt they piss themselves."

"Be easier to kill, that way."

"I hope so. Did you talk to Cletus?"

"You mean *Rocket?* Yeah, I called him," Devlin said. "He doesn't like Paddies, but he hates the dagos more, right now. He's in."

"Hitting the place together?"

"In-de-*pen*-dent-ly, he says. But yeah, at the same time."

"How many people is he bringing?"

"Fifty, if you can believe him."

"Fifty? That sounds like a pipe dream."

"Crack pipe," Devlin said, and snickered.

"Speaking of which, you think his 'bruthas' might try wasting us, like accidentally on purpose?"

"Not before they've taken care of Gallo. After that, I'd say all bets are off."

"We're playing for the city, then," Shaughnessy said, confirming it.

"High time, I'd say."

"Smart move would be to let the Rocket squad go in ahead of us. That way, we got them in a sandwich."

"Caught between corned beef and meatballs, eh?"

"They take the heavy hits and grind down Gallo's soldiers, leaving us to mop up after."

"Could work," Devlin said.

"If their asses show on time, or if they show at all."

"I think they'll show, however many make it. Cletus took it personal, wops shooting up his place."

"If it *was* them," Shaughnessy stated.

"Who gives a shite? We get the extra cannon fodder, either way."

"I told the boys they should be ready for a free-for-all. No limit."

"Long as we get out before the law drops in," Devlin said.

"Goes without saying, eh?"

"Speaking of the law, it come as a surprise to me that Greg O'Malley had a fix in with the Gallos."

"Coulda knocked me over with a feather," Shaughnessy agreed.

"It makes me stop and think about some others I could mention."

"Don't do it, though. Good thing is, once there's no more Gallos left to pay them, they'll come hat in hand to see whoever's running things."

"Which would be us," Shaughnessy said.

"The very same."

"We'd best not feck it up then, brother."

"Never crossed my mind."

"You wanna flip for who puts Papa Vinnie down?"

"Whoever sees him first?" Devlin suggested.

"And the loser buys the first two rounds at Flannery's."

"I'll drink your whiskey any day."

"We'd best be heading out to Black Rock, then," Shaughnessy said. "I'd hate to miss the party altogether."

"Just be fashionably late to make our entrance."

Shaughnessy picked up his M4 carbine from the floor beside his chair and took it with him as he started for the exit.

Devlin would have plenty of spare magazines collected with the other gear, same mags used by the M16 and AR-15 variants. His backup weapons were a SIG Sauer P239 chambered for .40 S&W rounds, tucked in a horizontal holster at the small of his back, and a bone-handled switchblade he'd honed to razor sharpness, thirsty for a taste of blood.

It had been six—no, almost *seven* months—since Shaughnessy had shot a man, and that one managed to survive, though with a crucial lesson learned. This night, he didn't plan on leaving any of his enemies alive. He would go down in history, with Devlin, as the Mick who made a comeback, taught the Mafia a thing or two and made it stick.

Assuming they got through the night alive.

Clinton Street, East Side, Buffalo

ROCKET HAD NOWHERE near the fifty gunners he had promised to the Irishmen. Barely half that, if the truth be told, but they were strapped to hell and back, ready to rumble. Anyway, no harm had ever come from lying to a honky. It was standard ops around the 'hood.

It was full dark outside now, and his gangstas were itching to go. They'd scrounged up five cars, counting Rocket's Caddy STS, the cool Seville Touring Sedan. He would be riding shotgun—make that AK-47—with his four best men, and let the others follow in a righteous convoy over to the Black Rock hideaway where Vinnie Gallo reckoned he could hide.

Another white man's dumb idea.

Rocket was thinking of a movie he had seen years ago, with Spencer Tracy and a bunch of other honkies in it. Tracy was supposed to be a one-armed soldier, come looking for his best friend in some dinky town out west. You knew it was fantasy right off, because his friend was Japanese and this was just a few weeks after World War II. Turned out a bunch of other honkies killed the Asian, naturally, so the one-armed guy started kicking ass.

Bad Day at Black Rock, it was called. Now Rocket was about to make the sequel.

Bad Night at Black Rock, yeah, for anybody standing up with Gallo when the Clinton Street Commandos hit his pad.

Twenty-four men, besides himself, including two peewees he'd brought along to round the number off. One of them was just fifteen, but what the hell. He had to bust his cherry sometime, right? Rocket had personally shown him how to use a MAC-10, and supplied the hardware. All the peewee had to bring along was balls.

How many Gallo soldiers waited for them at their destination? Rocket couldn't guess, but this was all about respect and reputation. If he let the ofays kill his men without a reason in the world, and did nothing about it, Rocket knew he might as well pack up and move to Punk Town, sell his bootie on the street to any creep who came along.

He damn sure wouldn't be a man.

Last weapons check, before they started rolling. Everyone was jitter-jiving as he moved along the line, inspecting hardware, making sure they had the safeties on for driving across town, reminding them to keep the guns down, out of sight, so no one saw them, freaked and called the po-po. Rocket wouldn't mind dusting some cops, the way he felt right now, but if it kept him from the Gallos, that was out.

"All right," he said at last. "Y'all know where we's goin'. Take the thruway west, then north along the river. Watch the signs an' keep the car ahead of you in sight, but don't bunch up. Don't wanna look like some jive-ass parade. Let's do it!"

They were piling into cars a second later, really *doing* it, with Rocket's Caddy leading as they rolled out of the warehouse he'd selected as their staging point. Nothing could stop them now, unless one of his men did something stupid. Knowing what it meant to him, to all of them—and what he'd do to anyone who failed him—Rocket didn't think they'd screw it up.

Bad Night at Black Rock, baby. Coming to you live, in ever-loving black-and-white.

Detroit Metropolitan Airport

ZOE ALMOST DIDN'T make the call. She was afraid, on one hand, and embarrassed on the other. Frightened that she might catch Johnny in the middle of some life-or-death activity, maybe distract him at a crucial moment. Worse yet, have the call be traced and lead the enemy to Johnny—or to her. As for embarrassment, she'd made a damned fool of herself in Buffalo, had nearly died and taken Johnny with her, plus his scary friend with the gigantic rifle.

Jesus, what a day!

And all she had to show for it was Johnny's word that he *believed* her brother had been murdered, that she might never recover his remains for burial. He'd tried to break the news gently, but it had sickened Zoe. It had scarred her soul.

She called him, anyway, using a landline in the terminal, so that a trace wouldn't lead back to her directly. She was *that* smart, anyway. If someone traced the call from Johnny's end, somehow, they'd have to reach the airport, search both terminals, eyeball thousands of people who were flying in and out or meeting planes.

Good luck with that. Her flight was leaving in an hour, for Seattle. Where she'd go from there was anybody's guess.

Not home. Not yet.

She didn't have his number memorized, but read it off her cell phone, tapping out the digits with her head cocked, the old-fashioned handset wedged against her ear. It would have made her skin crawl the previous day, thinking of all the people who had pressed that plastic to their faces, but the thought of catching something from a telephone didn't intimidate her now.

Screw that. She had survived the freaking Mafia.

So far.

His phone rang, Zoe thinking she'd be satisfied with voice mail, but he answered on the second ring. "Hello?" It was a cautious tone; no way he could have recognized the number she was calling from.

"I had to thank you one more time," she said.

"You really didn't."

"Yes. You saved my life. You almost died."

"Not even close," he lied.

"Hey, I was there."

"I had an angel on my shoulder," Johnny said.

"Some angel. How's he doing?"

"Great. I'll call you when it's settled. You know…safe."

"You think it ever will be?"

"I'd bet my life on it."

"Don't do that. Please. For me, don't."

"You don't cash out in a game like this," he said. "Be safe. I'll call you."

"Johnny, I—"

The buzzing dial tone cut her off. Zoe hung up and headed toward her gate, uncertain now of what she'd meant to say in parting. Likely something stupid, rash, impulsive. Hopeless. Getting life mixed up with modern fairy tales where a private saved ladies in distress and they all lived happily ever after.

All except her brother, dead and gone forever.

And the whole lifesaving thing had been an imposition, hadn't it? No matter what he said, being polite, she'd very nearly gotten Johnny killed for no good reason other than her own pigheadedness. Trying to fantasize some great relationship from that jump-start was worse than foolish. It was crazy.

So, forget him. If and when he called, she would accept his report and add a bonus to his final payment. If he *didn't* call, then she would wait a week or two, and try to get in touch once more. Try to find out if he had made it back from Buffalo alive.

And light a candle for him, if he hadn't.

She could do that much, at least.

Black Rock, Buffalo

"AN INTERESTING LADY," Bolan said, as Johnny stowed his cell.

"I guess."

"Something to think about, another time."

"Don't worry. My head's in the game."

Johnny had found the Black Rock hardsite the old-fashioned way, through property records, then they'd trailed some stragglers over from North Forest Acres to clinch it. The surrounding wall prevented them from counting heads, but cars were going in, and none were coming out. Smart money said the godfather was in.

Now all they had to do was root him out, deal with his soldiers in the process and come out alive somehow.

The usual.

They'd parked a block downrange, watching the only gate that granted access to the property. Two goons were stationed just inside, no hardware showing, but it would be readily accessible. Ramming the gate would trash their car, which meant they had to find a spot to scale the wall, hoping there weren't dogs inside, or soldiers standing by to pick them off.

Lousy odds, but what other kind were there in this game?

"The east side's nice and dark," Bolan said, reaching up to switch off the rental's dome light.

"Suits me," Johnny replied, then added, "Hold on. Here comes company."

Headlights approached from the west, off Tonawanda, half a dozen cars in convoy formation. Bolan watched them draw closer, but couldn't tell from his position if their occupants were white or black. Not that it mattered, either way, as long as they provided a distraction and did everything within their power to reduce the Gallo forces penned up in the hardsite.

The lead car pulled up to the gate, pinning the guards inside with high beams, the driver blowing its horn. Someone leaned out on the passenger's side, a white face under sandy hair, and shouted something at the watchmen. Not impressed, one of the mafiosi yelled back, with a middle finger raised to punctuate his comment. Bolan saw the point car's shotgun rider duck back out of sight, then pop back with some kind of bulky-looking pistol that turned out to be full-auto when he sprayed a wild burst toward the gate.

Too hasty with the shots, he missed one guard entirely, while the other staggered off and out of sight, clutching an arm. In seconds flat, both mafiosi on the inside were returning fire, one with a pistol, while the other—still with two good hands—blasted the lead car with a semiauto shotgun, putting out its headlights.

"That's our cue," Bolan said, going EVA a heartbeat later, with the Milkor MGL slung low across his back, the Spectre M4 in his hands. Johnny was right behind him with his Steyr AUG, ready for anything except defeat.

Gunfire was hammering the walled estate's sole entrance as they ran through shadows to the east side of the wall. Eight feet, with no barbed wire on top of it to spook the neighbors, but there could be something else up there—motion detectors, maybe, that would signal any penetration to the big house at the center of the wooded property. There'd been no time for any kind of recon, just the satellite shots on Johnny's laptop, but it had to do for now.

With Irish rebels at the gate, Gallo's attention would be focused there. Whether the shooters from South Buffalo got through or not, they would have served their purpose for the moment. Any Gallo soldiers they took down were icing on the cake.

And Bolan was about to cut himself a slice.

14

"What the hell is that?" Gallo demanded.

Jerry Portoghesi cocked his head, frowning. "It sounded like—"

A sudden roar of guns erupted, after the sound of a car horn blaring in the middle distance, maybe from the gate. Gallo was on his feet before he realized he was moving, rushing to the paneled west wall of his study, while he snapped at Portoghesi.

"Get your ass out there and help the others!"

"Vin, I'm not a soldier," the man complained. "I never have been."

"So, tonight you grow a pair. Move it!"

As Portoghesi fled the study, Gallo ran his fingers down a deep groove in the paneling and found the small catch hidden there. He released it, swung a section of the wall aside on silent hinges, to reveal a small but well-stocked private arsenal.

Inside the felt-lined cubbyhole he kept a Heckler & Koch HK416 assault rifle and a Benelli M1 Super 90 semiautomatic shotgun. Three semiauto pistols—Colt, Glock and Beretta—hung beside the long guns from pegs through their trigger guards. A drawer beneath the weapons held spare magazines and ammo still in boxes.

First thing, he took a Hagor bulletproof suit jacket from its hanger on the inside of the hidden door, and slipped it on. It weighed about eight pounds, but what the hell. Once it was buttoned, he was fairly well protected from his shoulders to his hips.

Next, Gallo chose the 12-gauge, since he'd never been a great shot with a rifle. He could squeeze off seven rounds of double 0 within three seconds, if it came to that, and never mind the pinpoint aiming. Put it out there, forty-odd pellets, each .33 caliber, throwing a lead storm at any dumb bastard who thought he could take Vinnie Gallo.

He grabbed the Glock for backup, stuck it in the waistband of his slacks, then started stuffing his pocket with magazines for the pistol, and spare shotgun shells. Whatever happened next, no one would ever say the godfather of Buffalo had died from lack of shooting back.

Then, outside. He hadn't piled the hardware on to sit and cower in his study. If his *consigliere* found the guts to pitch in, how could *il padrino* fail to do his part?

Lead by example, right.

And if he made it to the damned garage, hop in a ride and get the hell away from there.

He was a brave man, not an idiot.

Why be a martyr, if he had a chance to live and fight another day?

It sounded like a full-scale war outside as Gallo left his study, moving down a corridor with artwork that had cost a bundle hanging on both walls. He wasn't what you'd call a connoisseur, but knew the kind of paintings that he liked—and what appreciated, gaining value over time.

All useless, if he got his ass shot by whoever in hell was after him tonight.

He didn't even try to work that out. Between the pricks who'd killed Joe Borgio, the Clinton Street Commandos and the Irish in South Buffalo, he had enough headhunters after him to keep him guessing.

Bottom line: the only thing he cared about was getting out alive.

THE WALL WAS easy, once the lookouts were distracted. Bolan and his brother scrambled over, found nothing atop the wall to slow them down and dropped onto the estate grounds in shadow. If there'd been roving patrols in place, the firefight at the gate had drawn them to join the action. No dogs barking, and the soldier took that as another lucky break. If they had triggered some kind of alarm inside the house…well, they'd be dealing with that soon enough.

The grounds reminded Bolan of a wooded park—or the kill zone around the Niagara Adventure Theater. Not thick woods, but enough trees standing tall and casting shadows that could conceal a lurking enemy prepared to fire on anything that moved. It would take stern discipline to stay in place and wait it out while their comrades were fighting to keep out the Irish, but Gallo might have a few soldiers like that.

Or the Bolan brothers might meet a coward hiding out.

And being frightened didn't mean he wasn't dangerous.

They moved toward the house, cautious, but making decent time. The Executioner had no idea how long the gate would hold, but if one raider got inside there'd be a button that could open it. Bolan was tempted to go back and help, but had his own agenda that was top priority.

When they were thirty yards beyond the fence, he saw more Gallo soldiers coming from the house, some running, six riding a pair of golf carts, three men to a car, all armed with long guns. Sending in the cavalry, or something like it. At the same time, shouts and creaking, grinding sounds told him the gate was opening. He glanced back, saw two members of the home team using muscle to delay it, until one was shot down and the other ran for cover.

"Gets worse now," Bolan said.

"Or better," Johnny answered.

As he spoke, he raised his Steyr, sighted, squeezed the trigger once. Downrange, one of the golf carts veered off course, its driver slumped over the steering wheel. The passengers were shouting, trying to correct its course, as Johnny turned back to his brother.

"Helps if they can't hold the gate," he said.

"Good thinking," Bolan replied, and glanced toward the big house. Every window he could see was lit up, as if they had some kind of party or reception going on. Huge power bill next month, but if they played their cards right, Vinnie Gallo wouldn't be around to pay it. Hell, who knew? The place might even be condemned.

Just like its owner, from the moment that he'd tangled with the Executioner.

"Yo, MAN! THEY started widout us!" Little Puppet said.

"Jus' like I planned," Rocket replied. "Get in behind them ofays quick, now, 'fore they shut the gate again."

Little Puppet did as he was told, gunning the Caddy STS toward Gallo's open gate, where guns were popping and the fight was going down. Rocket was ready with his AK-47, window lowered, sorry to sacrifice the Cadillac, but he could always get another ride. Your reputation, once they yanked that out from under you, forget it.

White guys on his right. They didn't look Italian to him, necessarily, but Rocket wasn't in the mood to check IDs. They gawked at him as if they'd never seen a brother in their lives, standing over a third guy on the ground whose head was mostly blown away and spilling tapioca on the grass. They hoisted guns, and Rocket let them have it, spent brass pouring out of the ejector port, feeling a bullet whisper past his face so near he could detect its heat.

Shit, that was close!

The Caddy was passing the honkies now, and both of them were still standing, firing back at him, until his last burst caught one in the hip and took his leg out, dropping him like someone's busted mannequin. The other man crouched, kept on shooting, Rocket shouting curses back at him and twisting in his seat, the angle wrong for a right-hander on the drive-by.

They were taking hits from all sides now, but Little Puppet held the Caddy steady, roaring down the driveway toward the big house, Rocket's soldiers coming on behind them. Here and there, a car had slewed off to the side, shot through, and there were bodies scattered all around, some lying still, others moving around as if they were hurt real bad, but still not giving up the ghost.

"Shit, man!" The fear was audible in Little Puppet's voice, but he kept driving. In the backseat, Rocket's men were firing from their open windows, maybe hitting something, maybe wasting precious rounds they'd wish for in another minute. At the house, suckers were ducking, dodging, shooting back and forth at one another, firing in and out of the lit windows. Rocket even saw a couple of them grappling on the lawn, as if they'd run out of bullets and decided they should tear each other limb from limb, bare-handed.

Crazy.

"Keep on!" he barked at Little Puppet, just before a slug came through the Caddy's windshield. The peewee's head snapped back, the side toward Rocket vaporized. There was no way to steer without a brain, for sure, but they kept rolling straight somehow, regardless, Little Puppet's dead foot on the gas, until they hit the mansion's steps and stalled.

"Out of the car!" Rocket ordered, but his men had figured that out for themselves, already bailing, crouched behind the Caddy's open doors for cover. Rocket felt as if he was playing *Doom* for real, but in this world his AK magazine was empty and he had to ditch it, swapping in a full one, while bullets flew thick and fast around him.

Screw it.

Leaping to his feet, he rushed the mansion's entrance and shot the dead bolt into tatters. He kicked the door open, crouching, seeing shadows duck around inside and chasing them with short full-auto bursts.

"Yo, Vinnie!" Rocket shouted from the threshold. "Dey's Commandos in the house!"

CRACKING THE GATE had cost him one man dead, another wounded, but Kevin Shaughnessy took the losses in stride. This was war, and losses were to be expected. Even so, it hurt when Brian Devlin fell, gut-shot and thrashing on the lawn, before he'd taken three steps from his car.

Sprawling beside his oldest friend, lying in Devlin's blood, Shaughnessy peered into his eyes while bullets rattled overhead. Their boys were giving back as good as they received, but they were still outnumbered, still the underdogs.

"Kev," Brian gurgled, drooling crimson, "get in there an' kill them feckers!"

"You hold on, hear me?" Shaughnessy replied.

"Don't think…I can," Devlin gasped. Then he coughed a gout of blood and shivered like a junkie kicking it cold turkey, clutching his friend's hand with force enough to crack the knuckles.

And he died.

Shaughnessy exploded, picking up his M4 carbine as he rose to one knee, looking for a target, any target, to receive his raging grief.

Before he found one, ramped-up firing at the gate drew his attention back there, and he saw more vehicles arriving. Not police yet, but a motley convoy rolling in, all of the faces visible through open windows black and brown. The other gang arrived, and they'd obviously come to party, muzzle-flashes winking from the windows of their pimped-out rides as they came charging toward the Gallo mansion.

"More, the merrier," he muttered to himself, then Shaughnessy was off and running toward the east side of the house, where he had seen a patio and barbecue. That normally meant sliding doors, a lot of glass and easy access once you strafed it with a few full-auto rounds. He wasn't passing Vinnie Gallo off to another gang if he could help it. Not with Devlin's blood fresh on his hands.

Some injuries required a personal response, and this was one of them.

Take out a brother, and you paid for it in blood.

He reached the patio with half a dozen of his men behind him, wasn't sure what had become of the remainder, and there wasn't time for him to think about it. Two of Gallo's men were coming through the sliding doors as he arrived, both armed with Uzi submachine guns. Shaughnessy caught one with half a dozen rounds, then ducked and rolled before the other had a chance to nail him. He came up firing, howling like a madman when his second target hit the paving stones, all rubbery and spastic.

Clear to storm the house, he charged ahead, afraid to turn to see if any of his boys were following, but not caring any longer. If he had to do the job alone, so be it.

He would meet the rest of them in hell, and they would have a high old time.

ON THE MANSION'S west side, Bolan found a door that had a window in its upper half. Beyond the glass, a kitchen sparkled underneath fluorescent lights. There was no sign of anybody moving when he checked that window or the one he supposed had to be above a sink. The door was locked, of course, but that was no impediment.

"One size fits all," he said, retreating to a safe range for the Milkor MGL.

"Blow it," his brother said.

He blew it, with a high-explosive round that struck the door dead center and disintegrated it. Bolan and Johnny charged in through the smoke and dust, ducked underneath a dangling piece of door frame, and were in the house before the shock waves from the blast had finished rattling through the Gallo mansion.

There was no one in the spacious kitchen, as expected, but there would be soon, if Gallo had enough men still remaining in the house to come and check on the explosion. Bolan wasn't waiting for them to arrive, preferring to go hunting on his own. He held the Milkor steady, with a buckshot round next up in its revolving cylinder, and led the way across the kitchen to another door, drawing them farther into the rambling house.

Johnny kept quiet as they moved into a corridor that ran north-south, with doors on either side. The first one Bolan opened brought them to a formal dining room that would accommodate some twenty-five or thirty guests around a long table with high-backed, leather-cushioned chairs. Again, there was nobody home, but Bolan could hear voices now, approaching from the south end of the hallway.

"You want to meet them here?" Johnny asked, standing ready with his Steyr.

"Might as well," Bolan replied.

He knelt to one side of the corridor, giving the enemy a smaller target as they suddenly came into view. The range was thirty yards or so; the targets, three unhappy shooters armed with long guns, stopping short at the sight of two grim-looking strangers on their turf. Bolan triggered the buckshot round before they could react, one blast from the Milkor equivalent to three 12-gauge shells packed with double 0 buck.

The pellets spread enough at that range to hit all three Gallo soldiers, though the loser in the middle took the worst of it, blown backward, airborne, leaving blood trails in the air. His sidekicks spun away in opposite directions, going down, and Johnny pinned them with a single round apiece to make it stick.

Ears cushioned by the Surefire plugs, Bolan heard Johnny ask, "If you were Gallo, where would you be?"

"Looking for a way out," he answered.

"Right. So, likely not a panic room."

"One exit, whether he decides to run or ride."

It clicked, their voices overlapping: "The garage."

PLANNING TO FLEE and actually getting out, Vinnie Gallo had discovered, were two very different things. He was barely out of his study when two of his men buttonholed him, asking where they ought to go, what they should do. Wanting the boss to do their thinking for them, as he always had.

He told them, "Get into the fight and hold the line," with a vague nod toward the front door of the mansion, where the racket was increasing. Gallo's goons looked nervously at one another, then took off to do as they'd been told.

Suckers.

An escort might have helped him reach the car, but it would also draw attention to him, which he definitely *didn't* want right now. If he could pass unnoticed through the chaos that surrounded him and snag a ride, he had a good chance of surviving.

If he kept his head down.

If the damned gate wasn't blocked.

He knew it wasn't *shut,* because his enemies had rolled up to the front door of his mansion like a trick-or-treat parade from hell. He'd heard the car horns, shooting, crazy yelling back and forth as if savages were closing in.

No problem.

Gallo had prepared for every possibility, including an escape plan just in case his wall was breached, his home invaded. Shortly after buying the estate, he'd had a tunnel dug between the mansion and its separate garage, completely reinforced with cinder blocks and I-beams. Entry to the tunnel from the house was through a storage closet with a false wall at the back. Its exit, at the other end, was through a metal cabinet in the garage's southwest corner.

Gallo loved that cloak-and-dagger nonsense.

This night, it just might save his life.

He made it to the closet without meeting any of his other soldiers on the way, unlocked it and was just about to step inside when someone called out from behind him, "Vinnie! Where ya going?"

Turning, he saw Al Cavallaro bustling toward him, with an Uzi submachine gun clutched beneath one arm. Gallo was fumbling in his head for an appropriate response when Cavallaro spoke again.

"Ya figure it was time to sweep the place, or what?" he asked, grinning in a sarcastic, sour way.

There was no point in bullshitting. "I'm getting out of here. You wanna come?" Gallo asked.

A blink from Cavallaro, then he said, "I thought ya'd never ask."

"Come on, then."

With Cavallaro behind him, Gallo stepped into the closet, found the hidden latch that held the secret door secure and opened it. A ten-foot flight of wooden steps descended into darkness, brightened when he flipped a light switch hidden underneath a shelf lined with jugs and bottles of cleaning supplies.

"We're going down there?" Cavallaro asked.

"I am," Gallo answered. "You can stay here, if you're claustrophobic."

"Hell, no. Let's get moving."

Pissed at being saddled with a nag, and wondering what he could do about it, Gallo started down the stairs, into the womb of earth.

"THIS JUST MIGHT be the worst freakin' idea you ever had," Mick Strauss declared.

"Nobody made you tag along."

"Hey, what's a partner for?"

I wonder, sometimes, Leo Kelly thought, but kept it to himself. They were within a hundred yards of Gallo's gate, and he could see it standing open, an unprecedented circumstance. Closer, he saw a body sprawled inside the opening, and then another. Gunfire, audible when they were still a quarter mile from the estate, was louder now, and punctuated by explosions.

"Holy—! It's World War III," Strauss said.

"Still time to bail," Kelly replied.

"Screw that. Let's do it!" As he spoke, Strauss jacked a round into the chamber of his Remington Model 870 shotgun, clutching the piece in a white-knuckled grip.

Kelly's own Remington—the improved Model 887 Nitro Mag—was propped beside him in the driver's seat, where he could reach it quickly once he'd stopped the Crown Victoria and jumped into the fight. He wasn't looking forward to it, but the call had come from Gallo that he needed help, and there was no way to avoid it, short of blowing off the godfather and hoping someone snuffed him before he issued orders for the rogue detectives to be whacked. All thoughts of Zoe Dirks had been driven from his mind.

A do-or-die job, and it still might work to their advantage, if their luck held. Granted, that was feeling shaky lately, but there were a couple ways it could play out to Kelly's personal advantage, so he wasn't giving up. Not yet.

One way to run it down, he and his partner happened on the battle site before the squeal went out and called for reinforcements to assist them. Drop whoever had invaded Gallo's space and save the ritzy neighborhood from low-rent lunatics, and they'd be heroes. Break it down another way, and if they had to take out Vinnie G., that act alone should cripple any claims that they were bought and paid for by the Mob.

A win-win situation, sure—as long as no one blew Kelly's head off in the meantime.

As for Mick, his kinks were getting old, had caused them trouble once too often. The department always got good mileage out of martyrs.

They were through the gate now, rolling past more corpses, swerving around cars that had been shot to hell and stalled out in the driveway. Checking out the battlefield, Kelly imagined this would be the end of TV anchors calling Gallo a "reputed" gangster. Anyone who thought this kind of shit went down by accident, outside a straight guy's house, would have to be a freaking idiot.

"You ready, partner?" he asked Strauss.

"Damn right!"

"Okay, then."

Kelly stopped the Crown Vic, switched its engine off and left the key in the ignition. If somebody bagged it, what the hell? There'd be a hundred squad cars on the property within the next ten minutes, anyway. He grabbed his shotgun, popped the door and rolled out onto neatly manicured grass, just as a bullet smashed the driver's window overhead.

15

Bolan set the house on fire before they left. It wasn't difficult: one 40 mm pyrotechnic round into the Electrolux ICON pro-style gas range as they passed through the kitchen and out, first detonation from the impact, then flames racing through the mansion's gas lines to the furnace, water heater and laundry room. A mass inferno from a single trigger stroke.

Bolan gave no thought to the soldiers who were trapped inside, the hanging art or lavish furnishings, the servants who'd be left without a paycheck in the morning. He was hunting Vinnie Gallo, and a little dose of hell on earth was waiting for whoever stood between him and his quarry.

"Won't be long before the cops and fire department show," his brother said.

"And Gallo knows it," Bolan answered. "If he's getting out, he can't afford to wait."

"What are the odds he's still inside?" Johnny asked, glancing back toward the mansion, all in flames.

"I couldn't tell you, but I won't take it for granted."

Bolan had glimpsed Gallo's garage on their approach, a five- or six-car building, well back from the house. There'd been no guards in evidence around it then, and he could see none now, in the light of the blazing funeral pyre that was the monster's second home. If he was wrong, and Vinnie Gallo wasn't running, taking out the cars was still a worthwhile move.

It meant nobody else could get away, except on foot.

The soldier had used three of the Milkor's six rounds in the mansion, and reloaded on the run now, with his shadow and Johnny's advancing like a pair of hulking giants on the lawn before them, from the firelight at their backs. The fight, from what he heard and saw, was focused on the house now, having moved on from the gate. A trail of shot-up cars and bodies lined the driveway, bloodstains glinting on the pavement and the short-cropped lawn.

They'd halved the distance from the mansion to the overgrown garage when another one of Gallo's golf carts zoomed out of the shadows there, charging across the grass in their direction. Bolan counted three men in the chunky vehicle, two firing as they came, the driver hunched over his steering wheel in kamikaze mode.

Johnny, diving for the turf, called back, "How many of those damned things does he have?"

Bolan ignored the question, snapped the Milkor to his shoulder, made target acquisition through the launcher's Armson Occluded Eye Gunsight, and sent an HE round downrange to meet the mini-charger. Its explosion stood the golf cart on its nose, its occupants ejected like a troupe of acrobats escaping from a clown car.

Bolan had the Spectre M4 ready as the tumbling bodies hit, stitching the nearest of them with a 3-round burst, while Johnny's AUG cracked lethal greetings at another of the trio. Number three was nimble, springing to his feet as if the crash was something he had practiced, but he'd dropped his piece somewhere along the way and came up empty-handed. Trying to correct that, he was digging underneath his jacket for a sidearm when the Spectre stuttered through its sound suppressor again and put him down.

Bolan and Johnny rose together and advanced toward the garage.

ROCKET WAS ROASTING, and didn't like it one damned bit. He'd lost his homeys somewhere, and now he couldn't find the ofay bastards he had come to deal with, either. Stumbling through a giant house on fire, he hardly knew which end was up, the fierce heat baking into him and making him feel dizzy as he lurched from room to smoky room.

Standing at one end of a hallway leading nowhere, Rocket realized that there had been no need for his gang to come here. The honkies were killing one another just fine without him. Behind him, something cracked deep in the house, a sound like fat logs in a fireplace. Something else gave out a moan, as if it was getting ready to collapse, and Rocket started moving down the corridor. Where to? He didn't have the first freaking idea.

How could he get lost in a goddamn *house,* for Christ's sake? He thought for a second. It was big, okay, but not *that* big. It wasn't like a freaking super mall or something. Find a door and get the hell out. Bust a window if you have to. Had to be a way out, or the people couldn't come *in.*

Where in hell had *he* come in? Another question Rocket couldn't answer if his life depended on it.

Which, he had begun to think, it might.

He wasn't scared of fire—had set a few himself, in fact, and watched them burn—but this was something else entirely. This was being stuck inside an oven with the goddamn broiler on, and no way out. And if a person thought *that* wasn't scary, he or she could think again.

The AK-47 dragged at Rocket's arms, twelve pounds of wood and metal getting hotter by the minute, so his palms were smarting where he held it. Rocket thought about discarding it, then wondered if he ought to blast an exit through one of the mansion's walls. He'd seen it done in movies, but you'd need an outside wall, and wouldn't there be doors and windows, anyhow, if you were standing next to one of those?

The way his luck was running, Rocket figured he'd likely shoot his way into a pantry or a bathroom, and it wouldn't be like something out of *Penthouse,* where he'd catch two smokin' hotties in the shower, lathering each other up. More likely find a dead guy on the toilet, smoldering, before the roof caved in and buried both of them.

In desperation, Rocket started sprinting down the hallway, wondering if it would ever end. He got his answer seconds later, as he came around a corner to confront a roaring wall of flame. The sound his throat made was a sob, mixed with a gasp for fading oxygen.

He turned, tried to retreat, and that was when the ceiling buckled, knocked him flat and pinned him there. No longer Rocket, and definitely frightened, Cletus Washington began to scream.

MICK STRAUSS WAS scared, which always pissed him off and made him mean. Some would have said that he was mean to start with—teenage hookers, for example—and he wouldn't have disputed it. But there were different kinds of mean, and at the moment he was *killing* mean.

The first thing that had gone wrong, aside from coming out to Gallo's place to start with, had been getting separated from his partner. Strauss had no idea where Leo Kelly was, or how they'd managed to lose track of each other. It occurred to him that Kelly might have ditched him purposely, but what would be the sense in that? Ten years together on the job, and all the stuff they'd done in tandem, forged some kind of bond.

If not, what was there in the world that anyone could count on?

Still…

He'd thought about just bailing, it was true. The minute he first missed Kelly, couldn't spot him anywhere nearby, Strauss had been tempted to run back, jump in the black Crown Vic and haul ass out of there. Not *really* leave, but duck away and hide somewhere until the SWAT guys started rolling in, then follow them back to the killing ground. Safer that way, but he'd decided that he couldn't live with it.

Now he was freaking stranded on his own and scared to death.

He'd shot one guy already—not a Gallo soldier, but black and wild-eyed, with an Uzi he was trying to reload when Strauss dropped him with buckshot from a range of twenty feet or so. Easy, and satisfying in its way, but he was still neck-deep in it, with no way out.

So, where in hell would Kelly go?

Strauss hoped he wasn't in the house, a flaming hulk now, radiating heat enough to blister paint on cars parked out in front, and singe the hair of bodies lying on the broad front steps. If Kelly was in there, Strauss hoped he had the common sense to shoot himself or do what firemen had advised him: face the flames and breathe as deeply as you can, searing your lungs and ending it before you wound up being cooked alive.

Bad news.

He couldn't check the house, regardless. Someone else would have to rake the ashes, hours or days from now. And if he couldn't find his partner, Strauss supposed the next best thing would be to corner Vinnie Gallo, tell the bastard to his face what it would cost him to get out of this in one piece, maybe even dodging major prison time.

Too late for that if Gallo was inside the mansion, blackened crispy-critters, but the godfather was wily. A survivor. Strauss imagined he would have an exit strategy, most likely more than one. Why let a fortress built to keep you safe become a trap?

While Strauss was thinking that, he saw a light go on in the garage.

JOHNNY THOUGHT THEY had it made, when half a dozen Gallo men came out of nowhere, firing on the run. Maybe they'd gathered in the dark woods, waiting to find out which way the fight was going, whether they should join in or retreat. Or maybe they'd been in it from the start, scattered, divided, then had found one another, closing ranks to try another round.

What mattered was the hot lead flying too damned close for comfort as he hit the turf with force enough to drive the air out of his lungs. Fighting to draw a breath, he raised his head to get a quick count on the enemy—seven, not six—and aim the Steyr in their direction. Firing prone meant Johnny had to push up on his elbows, giving them a larger target than he wanted to, but otherwise he couldn't use the AUG effectively.

Even then, a bullet hissing past his head made him flinch involuntarily. The 3-round burst that he'd meant to kill the shooter farthest to his right struck low, shattering femurs, and the guy pitched forward on his face, howling. A fourth round, through the cranium, silenced his voice for good, and Johnny moved on to another target.

His brother was doing his bit for the cause, and then some, with the Spectre M4 SMG, holding it sideways so the casket magazine wouldn't be jammed into the ground and force the muzzle skyward. Hot brass spit from the ejector port in handfuls, while the silenced weapon sputtered death downrange. Before Johnny lined up his second target, Mack had taken down two Gallo soldiers, his 9 mm Parabellum hollowpoint rounds inflicting hydrostatic shock on organs that the slugs themselves would never reach.

It was a hard and bloody way to die, but Johnny couldn't think of any nice ways if he tried.

He focused on the soldier in his sights and got it right this time, a short tattoo dead center on the running target's chest. The Steyr's 5.56 mm NATO rounds were tumblers, didn't mushroom like a hollow-point when penetrating flesh and bone, but turned end over end, deformed by impact in the process, plowing a god-awful wound channel. Striking a heart, they shredded muscle *and* drove slivers of the shattered sternum into the surrounding tissue, similar to shrapnel from a frag grenade.

Another Gallo soldier, down and out.

Mack beat him to the rest, his Spectre sweeping left to right across the dwindling skirmish line to cut them down. It wasn't disappointing, in the normal sense—Johnny derived no joy from killing, took no pride in it—but he preferred to hold up his end in a fight.

Rising, he checked the Steyr's transparent magazine by firelight, saw he'd used about two-thirds of it, and was preparing to replace it with a full one when a harsh voice called out from behind him.

"Freeze right where you are! Police!"

FOR A SECOND, Vinnie Gallo worried that he wouldn't get the latch inside the metal cabinet to open. It was sticking tight, and he regretted that he'd tried it only once since the escape route was completed. If the latch had rusted shut—

His momentary panic fled as he applied some extra pressure to the latch and forced it open. Swallowing the string of curses that had built up in his throat, he pushed through into the five-car garage, turned right at once and found the light switch with a minimum of fumbling. White fluorescent lights hummed overhead and bathed a row of brightly polished vehicles in a glow devoid of any warmth.

Standing in front of him, nearest to farthest, were a navy blue Cadillac CTS-V Coupe, a white Jaguar XJ full-size luxury saloon, a red Mercedes-Benz S-Class sedan, a silver Lexus GX midsize SUV and a cream-colored Rolls-Royce Phantom Coupé. Gallo loved each and every one of them, but didn't have a lot of time to dick around deciding which to pick.

"Get in the Caddy," he told Cavallaro. "I'll drive."

"Not so fast," a gruff voice stated, drawing Gallo's full attention to a side door that was standing open when it shouldn't be.

How the hell did I miss that? he asked himself, disgusted.

And he saw one of the dicks, Mick Strauss, half smiling at him, his complexion washed out by the overheads, some kind of fancy shotgun in his hands.

Gallo, holding his own 12-gauge, said, "Christ, I didn't think you'd make it. Where's your partner?"

Strauss gave a quick one-shoulder shrug. "Around here somewhere."

"You should go and find him," Gallo said. "It ain't exactly safe out there."

"You're telling me? I shot a black on your lawn. What's up with that?"

"Gate crashers," Gallo said. "There goes the neighborhood."

Strauss barked a laugh. "That's rich. Looks like you're taking off."

"Nothing to hang around for, is there?" Gallo asked him.

"I was thinking you could pay me, first, before you split. I'll hold my partner's half until I see him."

"Pay you *what?* Your monthly envelope isn't fat enough? Last job you did for me, you screwed it up so bad it's come to this. *You* should be paying *me,* you lousy—"

Strauss shot Cavallaro without warning, opened up his chest with buckshot, blowing him away, and jacked another round into the chamber as he swung his piece to cover Gallo.

"Jesus, man! What the hell'd you do that for?"

"Got your attention, didn't it?" the cop asked. "Now, then, about my payoff."

"How much you think I'm carrying?" Gallo asked, dry-mouthed, wondering if he could level his Benelli before Strauss squeezed off another round.

"I'm having second thoughts about it," he replied. "Thinking I'd rather be a hero than some two-bit dago's button man."

He raised the shotgun, and Gallo did all he could think of, turning so that Strauss would have to shoot him in the back, trusting the tailored ballistic jacket as he hunched his shoulders, ducking forward, praying that the buckshot wouldn't strike him in the head.

It felt like King Kong punching him, and there was thunder in his ears as Gallo slammed against the Caddy, spine and ribs on fire. But he was still alive, goddamn it, turning as he fell and firing twice with the Benelli semiauto, blasting Strauss off his feet and back out through the door he had entered.

Fighting for breath, Gallo lurched to his feet, slumped back against the pellet-dimpled CTS-V Coupe and tugged open the driver's door.

"LET ME GUESS," the cop said. "You two assholes are the ones who started all this."

Bolan stood silent, facing him, as Johnny spoke. "I'd guess *you* started it when you killed Joe Dirks."

"Oh, that."

"Which one are you?" Johnny asked. "Strauss or Kelly?"

"Leo Kelly, at your service. Mick's around here somewhere."

"Call him," Johnny said. "We'll have a square dance."

"I'm not in a sharing mood," Kelly replied. "For the record, which one of you pricks killed Greg O'Malley?"

Bolan broke his silence, asking, "Does it matter?"

"Not to me," Kelly admitted. "Say you both were in on it. Looks better that way, when I've got you tagged and bagged."

"Big hero," Johnny said. "Is that the plan?"

"Why not? I've spent enough time taking human garbage off the streets. I got some recognition coming."

"How's that reconcile with working for the Mafia?" Bolan asked.

"Nothing wrong with moonlighting."

"Or murder?" Johnny interjected.

"All depends on how you look at it. I mostly wasted pricks who had it coming anyway."

"And Joe Dirks?"

"You're a broken record, pal. That one should of minded his own beeswax."

"It doesn't bother you at all, does it?" Bolan asked.

"Nope. Can't say it does," Kelly replied.

"It bothers *me*," a voice said from the shadows, bringing Kelly's head around.

"The hell? Sarge? Listen, man—"

Kelly began to turn, raising his shotgun, but a pistol cracked once, twice, three times, the muzzle-flashes merging into one. Shot through, he fell almost at Bolan's feet, gasping the final microseconds of his life away.

"Sergeant Mahan," Bolan said to the tall and weary-looking man who stood before them.

"You," Mahan replied. "Is this your party?"

"I sent out the invitations," Bolan said. "B.Y.O.G."

"For guns. That's cute," Mahan replied. "Now, exactly what in hell am I supposed to do with you?"

"Your call," Bolan told him. "Whatever you decide—"

"You don't shoot cops. Yeah, I remember. Thanks for leaving that to me."

"You call this one a cop?" Johnny asked, pushing it.

"He used to be, I guess. None of us come out squeaky-clean."

"You've done all right, from what I hear," Bolan said.

Mahan glanced back toward the house in flames. "I couldn't root this out," he said. "The Gallos of this world get fat and sassy while I'm bagging two-bit losers."

"Saving lives," Bolan said.

Mahan eyed the body sprawled between them. "Not tonight."

Before Bolan could answer that, he heard the rumbling sound of a garage door opening behind him, turned and squinted in the glare of high-beam headlights as a sleek car hurtled toward them, engine snarling.

Johnny raised his Steyr without thinking, caught a fleeting glimpse of Vinnie Gallo's face behind the steering wheel before firing a short burst at the windshield. Then he dodged to his left, dropping and rolling, bobbing upright once more and leveling his rifle. His brother and the detective sergeant were unloading at the same time, rapid-firing at the Cadillac as it raced toward them, moving only when it was a matter of survival, in the final seconds.

Then the car was past them, homing on the distant gate, with Gallo still accelerating. Johnny held the Steyr's trigger down and tried to stay on target as he burned up half a magazine in no time, peppering the Caddy's trunk and bumper. Mahan's pistol *pop-pop-popped* in his two-handed grip, the cop forgetting that he had two felons right in front of him, focused as he was on halting Gallo's flight.

And for a moment, Johnny thought that Mack had given up. He'd let the Spectre drop and dangle from its shoulder sling, but then he raised the Milkor MGL, peering downrange through its reflex sight, the red-dot kind that helped pinpoint a target on the move. Then he began to fire, squeezing the

trigger slowly and deliberately, cranking off three rounds before he paused.

The Caddy took all three, a walking chain of blasts that
marched across its trunk lid, roof and hood like triple lightning strikes. They didn't stop the car immediately, but its
flaming hulk veered to the left and lost momentum, rolling
to a smoky halt before the fuel tank blew and spread a lake
of fire around the once-luxurious machine.

"Jesus!" Johnny couldn't have said if that was awe or simple
weariness in Mahan's voice. "You guys don't screw around."

"We can't afford to," Bolan replied.

"So, now what?" Johnny asked. "You lock us up?"

Mahan considered it, his eyes narrowing as he heard sirens
warbling in the distance.

"It means a lot of paperwork," he said at last. "Explaining
things I don't even pretend to understand."

"So, then…?"

"You have a ride around here somewhere?"

"Not too far," Bolan said.

"Then I'd suggest you get the hell away from here," Mahan
replied. "Give me time to come up with some kind of fairy
tale to cover this."

"You sure about this?" Bolan inquired.

"Not even. So you'd better haul ass while you can, before
I change my mind."

They hauled, without another word or backward glance.
The brothers scaled Gallo's wall not far from where they'd
entered the estate, clearing the grounds as cruisers, unmarked
cars and a SWAT van started rolling in, their red and blue
lights strobing, sirens winding down.

A block away, the Mercury sat waiting for a long ride back
to someplace safe.

Epilogue

"You'll get in touch with Zoe?" Bolan asked his brother.

"Try to, anyway. Or else she'll get in touch with me."

"What will you tell her?"

Johnny shrugged. "She knows her brother's gone. The hard part will be living with it."

"Maybe Mahan will come up with something."

"Maybe," Johnny said. He didn't sound convinced.

"You did a good job," Bolan stated.

"Like when you tell someone they've done their best, meaning they screwed things up with good intentions."

"No. Not meaning that, at all."

"I sucked you into this, because I couldn't handle it my-self."

"No shame in that."

"And I'm a cop-killer," Johnny reminded him.

"It isn't something you'll forget," Bolan said, "but there's no need to keep punishing yourself. O'Malley chose his road and reached the only end it could've had."

"You've never done it."

"There but for the grace of—"

"Yeah, I hear you. Doesn't make it any easier."

"It's not intended to. What time's your flight?"

"Nine thirty-seven, if you can believe it. I'll be lucky if we're in the air by ten-fifteen."

"Good to be home, though," Bolan said.

"I guess."

"You may want to consider laying off the field trips for a while."

"I hear you, bro'. I'm selling off my frequent-flier miles."

"I'll try to swing out that way, pretty soon."

"Be good to see you," Johnny said. "Without the rest of it, I mean."

Without the rest of it, Bolan thought, meaning endless war, bloodshed and the incessant threat of sudden death.

"Without that, right."

But something told the Executioner that he would never be without it. He, like Greg O'Malley and the rest, had picked a life path that was strewn with corpses, fraught with peril. He had chosen it with eyes wide-open, and he couldn't honestly pretend that he had no regrets. Or that he'd "win," whatever that meant, in the end.

But he would keep on fighting, sure.

It was the only way he knew to play the game.

* * * * *